Man

It's all One Big Thing

by

Steve Tyler

ISBN:

Ebook: 979-8-90224-055-6
Paperback: 979-8-90224-056-3
Hardcover: 979-8-90224-057-0

Published by:
Authors Publishing House
178 Broadway, 3rd Floor, #1343
New York, NY 10001, USA

Main Line: (855) 624-0155
Email: support@authorspublishinghouse.com

Table of Contents

The Gas can Incident

Susan, my wife, and I went on vacation to South Carolina for a week and left two of our sons, Jimmy and Jack at home to manage the property. And we had a wonderful time. We enjoyed simple pleasures—going for walks on the beach, collecting seashells, fresh seafood. Very relaxing.

All seemed well when we returned. But I did notice a couple of things out of place. There was a small lamp that was broken, but neither son had any idea how this possibly could have happened. All right, I let that go. The other thing I noticed was a gas can sitting on the front porch which did not belong to us. I questioned Jimmy, and he said a friend had run out of gas and they had used that gas can to rescue him. Subsequently the gas can was forgotten and left on the porch. I declared it was now my gas can since it was left on my property. No one objected.

A few days later Susan and I were doing some lawn work and I thought I would try out the new gas can. It had the kind of spout I like—a long one which makes it easier to pour gas into the lawn mower versus the new type which have very short spouts as an apparent safety feature. It is my understanding, according to National Public Radio, that three people in America spilled gasoline with a long spout can, causing three fires somewhere in the country. So regulations now prohibit long spouts on gas cans. Well, my new can had a long spout, but it did have a safety feature: a spring loaded device at the end of the spout which needed to be twisted to allow the spout to open. This is apparently to prevent the spout from being inadvertently aimed at the wrong place, which could start a conflagration of some sort. The spout contained a spring which looked something like this:

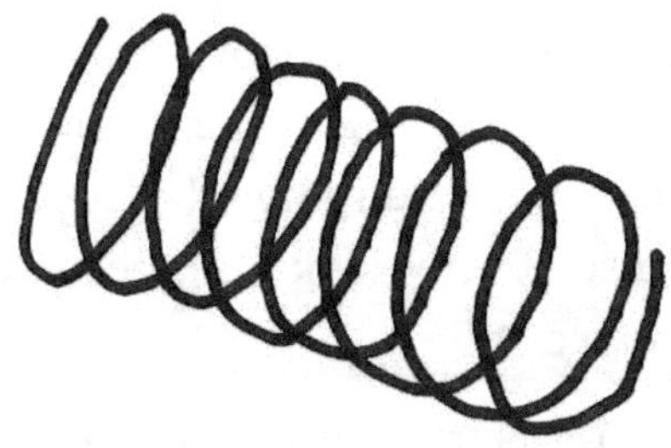

Well, I really loved the long spout on that can but I thought I could make it perfect by removing the spring safety device. So I started taking it apart but it seemed to be locked in place somehow. In order to get a better understanding of the engineering of the device, I held it up to my face and looked directly down the spout. Then I did what any sensible Hoosier would do, I twisted the end of the spout with some pliers and it came off. The spring inside then shot a bullet shaped object at very high velocity into my right eye.

Now I have a pretty high pain tolerance, but I have to admit that this really hurt. I yelled "FUCK!" and turned to Susan and said, as calmly as possible, "I think I just shot my eye out." Susan is a nurse and she quickly assessed that my eye was still in my head and she gave me her normal advice: "It'll be okay, don't worry about it." "Okay," I said. I tried the new altered gas can. It worked perfectly. The gasoline flowed from the can with incredible ease. I felt kind of gratified. Nevertheless, deep down I suspected my right eye was messed up. So I locked that thought away in my titanium-like minimization/denial system.

Now, I am a Clinical Social Worker. One of my monthly duties at that time was to provide services to the Boone County Jail with my friend and associate, Dr. Jerry Sheward. We went to the jail monthly to do psychiatric examinations on inmates—inmates who were psychotic as well as ones who were simply depressed by being in jail and thought they might want to kill themselves, etc. I enjoyed going to the jail with Jerry. I frequently referred to Jerry as "my psychiatrist," which amused my friends more than I felt necessary. In any case, I told Jerry the story about my eye and how, since the incident, I would see flashes of light when I moved my eyes quickly. He gave me a look of concern and said I might have a detached retina and that I should probably have somebody look at it, because if untreated it could lead to blindness in that eye.

Okay, this suggestion penetrated my titanium-like minimization/denial system so I scheduled an appointment with my optometrist, Dr. Gloria Jennings. Due to the nature of the problem, she wanted me scheduled the next day. During the examination I told her I was seeing flashes of light and she said "Oh my, that's not good." I didn't like the sound of that. She examined my right eye closely and soon said she was going to refer me to a specialist. I asked who and she quietly said, "Eye Surgeons of Indiana." I didn't like the sound of that either. Dr. Jennings tried to reassure me. She said they probably wouldn't have to do surgery, but they should look at it. "Okay."

I arranged an appointment with Eye Surgeons of Indiana. The appointment was at four o'clock on a Friday, so I blocked out my office schedule from three o'clock on to allow myself forty-five minutes to get to Eye Surgeons of Indiana. I managed a psychiatric clinic at that time which can be a messy and chaotic scene, as you can imagine. So, as the time approached to leave for my appointment at Eye Surgeons of Indiana a patient unexpectedly showed up at the office, crying, demanding, making a scene. I helped to unwind the situation as quickly as possible to hit the road for my appointment. As it turns out, I managed to leave thirty minutes later than what I had planned for my drive to Eye Surgeons of Indiana.

I raced down the interstate fearing that I would be late for two reasons: I knew that medical providers have little tolerance for patients showing up late for four o'clock appointments on Friday. Also, my wife Susan planned to be there, no doubt on time, and I did not want to frustrate her. So, I proceeded to attempt a new land speed record from my office in Lebanon, Indiana to the northeast side of Indianapolis where the Eye Surgeons of Indiana office is located. As I sped, I glanced in my rear view mirror and did a visual assessment of myself. I noticed that my hair was unusually long and unkempt. It seemed even more gray than normal. I really wished I had gotten a haircut. The crisis in the outpatient office as well as my concern that I was considerably late for this appointment had visibly affected my overall appearance. I felt and looked like I was fighting a losing battle.

Amazingly, however, I got to Eye Surgeons of Indiana at around five minutes after four—just in time to be seen. The first part of the interaction involved filling out paperwork about my insurance, medical history, medications, and an advanced directive should I accidentally slip into a coma while under the care of Eye Surgeons of Indiana. Now my wife Susan sat with me in front of the receptionist who was presenting these documents. Susan was dressed in a white lab coat—she is a nurse at Community Hospital located just next to Eye Surgeons of Indiana. She presented herself as perfectly groomed, poised, and professional. On the other hand, I was disheveled, and frankly angry that I had been detained at work by an unruly patient, which fed into my sense that my job was an unending stream of complaints and "crises" which too frequently seeped into my consciousness as evidence that humanity is out of control and that these incidents created other inconveniences, including delaying me from important appointments, like this one, at Eye Surgeons of Indiana.

But another unfortunate problem occurred. I left my reading glasses in my car so I could not read the paperwork being presented. So the process of completing the paperwork involved Susan reading parts to me, explaining, pointing out where I should sign, and me arguing with her saying things like: "This is stupid," "Why would I need to sign something like this?" "This doesn't make any sense to me," "What's wrong with this place?" etc. I was visibly agitated. Susan politely asked me to settle down. She reassured me that things would be okay. This was all observed by the receptionist whose job is not just to get forms signed. An equally important part of the receptionist's job is to inform the treating physician about how the next patient they are going to see is BEHAVING. And I wasn't behaving well at all.

So, I was taken to the exam room and my first encounter was with an intern. She asked me why I was there and I told her: "I shot my eye with a device from a gas can and my psychiatrist told me I should come and get it checked out." Now I thought that referring to Jerry Sheward as "my psychiatrist" was a funny thing to say, but of course, the intern had no idea what I was referring to, and I could see this in her eyes. So I quickly tried to correct myself: "I work with a psychiatrist and we evaluate inmates in the Boone County Jail and he told me I should have my eye checked out." This clarification did not seem to help so I just let it go.

Susan was with me in the interview. She continued to look like a perfect medical angel: uniformed, well groomed, every hair in place, patient, completely competent and organized. And, as the world knows, she is ten and a half years younger than I am. She is also exceptionally attractive for her age. Or, for any age, for that matter. The intern turned to Susan and asked: "Are you his daughter?" Susan lost her cool here and said: "NO! I'm his WIFE!" The intern looked a little surprised and said, "Okay." We moved on.

So the intern began some questioning including "How much alcohol do you drink?" I replied: "I like to have a glass of wine with my daughter on Saturday nights." The intern didn't react to my sarcasm and continued. The intern looked deeply into my right eye with a bright light, and held it there for what seemed like a very long time. The intern finally told us that I had a "vitreous detachment." This simply means that the back of my right eye was no longer attached to anything. She said, "This happens to everyone eventually, if you live long enough. Usually around age eighty-five. There is nothing we can do about it. Don't worry, your eye won't fall out." The intern told us that the supervising eye surgeon would have to come in and check her work.

Well the supervising eye surgeon came in and began to ask his questions. But he was not talking to me. He asked Susan: "Are you his caretaker?" Susan, irate, says "NO, I'm his WIFE!" In any case, he continued to ask her the questions, as if I wasn't present. I could actually feel my stature shrinking from the awareness that these people, despite our clarifications, were viewing me as a dementia patient and Susan as my caregiver. I realized that trying to explain that I don't have dementia would probably just make matters worse. I decided to simply capitulate and to add this experience to the long list of self-deprecating and humiliating stories that I have catalogued in my mind over the past 60 years. And like the other stories on that long list, after a few days, it seemed surprisingly amusing.

The Wedding

"If I go, do I have to see Hallie?" Jeff Hill said.

"Yes Jeff, that's part of the deal when you go to a wedding. You'll be with me, the best man. Yes, so you are going to have to socialize with Hallie, the bride," I said. Jeff had unfavorable feelings about Hallie--not necessarily that he didn't like her. It was worse than that. He thought she was boring. For Jeff, boredom was life's unforgivable sin. Despite Jeff's concerns, Jeff nevertheless agreed to go to the wedding.

So, in May 1985 Jeff and I flew to San Francisco to attend the wedding of Kim McDonald and his fiancé, Hallie Freeman. After arrival, we took custody of a rental car--a 1983 Camaro convertible. We claimed our room at the Motel 6 on Industrial Boulevard in Wayward, which was just west of San Jose and on the coast. We spotted a small bar called *The Working Man's Friend* across the street from the motel and had a couple of beers to celebrate our arrival in the Bay Area. We soon realized we were a half hour off schedule and quickly took off to Kim and Hallie's apartment for a meeting to discuss wedding plans.

On the way, I described the family scene we would be walking into at the wedding planning session. "Hallie is really twitchy and O.C.D. about the wedding plans. Her mother, Minneray, is a control freak who is generally cranky and disagreeable. Stanley, the father, is a sit in the corner kind of guy, barely visible. He's worn out on Minneray. The old guy is spending his senior years sleeping on his sailboat in a Marin County Marina just to avoid being alone with her."

"If you look close enough, all families are kind of nuts." Jeff replied.

"Probably so." I said.

We arrived at Kim and Hallie's apartment, about thirty minutes late. We made our introductions which were mostly friendly, except for Minneray who declined to make eye contact with Jeff and me when Hallie introduced her. Following introductions, Minnaray asked for an explanation for our tardiness: "Hallie informed me that you would be here at three o'clock. We have been waiting on you for a half hour. We have a lot of business to discuss. Can you explain why you are so late, and so rude?"

Jeff injected himself: "Mrs. Freeman, I apologize. I can assure you that we intended no offense to you or Hallie. Steve and I were delayed by conditions beyond our control."

"Can I ask what circumstance delayed you?" Minneray asked.

"You certainly can." Jeff replied.

"……..Well what was it?" Minnaray again asked, becoming more frustrated.

Jeff replied, "We were thirsty and stopped for a couple of beers after we checked into our lodging. We felt this was an important thing to do, to slow down a moment to contemplate the wonderful ritual to take place tomorrow and the satisfaction of seeing Kim, one of our best friends, marry your beautiful daughter. I realize that this may not be a completely satisfactory explanation, but to Steve and me, this was our attempt to further sacralize the moment. Thank you so much for being patient."

"What do you mean by 'sacralize?' " Minnaray asked.

"Well…that means 'to make sacred,' " Jeff said.

"Then why didn't you just say that? We send you kids off to college and you come back with nothing but fancy words to try to impress everyone. Well, I'm not impressed. I'm really not the slightest bit impressed."

Stanley was accustomed to serving as a firewall for Minneray. He coyly intervened and quietly suggested to Minnaray that we move on to the wedding plans.

"All right, but from now on, everyone needs to comply with my plans, I mean Hallie's plans, for the wedding."

Well, the meeting took fifteen minutes. The detailed plans merely consisted of showing where we would each stand. The couple would be married on a bluff overlooking the Pacific Ocean with a reception at the clubhouse of a nearby condo. Nothing complicated.

The evening came and Kim, Jeff, and I decided to have a bachelor party, for three. The matter came to the attention of Minneray: "There is no good reason for a bachelor party. You three can just stay in tonight. I think that would be best," she said.

"Mrs. Freeman," I said, "I appreciate your advice, but the three of us have discussed the matter and we all agree that on the eve of the wedding, Kim should feel the support and love of his male friends. He needs to feel our admiration for his willingness to take on this deep commitment not only to Hallie, but to her entire family. Tomorrow is a day to be mindfully anticipated as well as warmly remembered."

"Do you guys ever just talk like normal?" Minnaray asked.

"Mrs. Freeman, don't you sometimes think that 'normality' is not real, it is an imaginary ideal. It may simply be heuristic," I said.

"I really don't care to deal with you people tonight," she uttered. Then she walked away.

"Thank you Minneray. It was good seeing you." I said.

So the three of us hopped into the 1983 Camaro and full throttled it to a friendly looking place we had spotted in Wayward. The sign in front of the club looked like this:

We told our waitress, Bambi, that Kim was getting married the next day and we wondered if there was anything available at *Leave It to Beavers* for men in this situation. Bambi told us that the girls like to "smush" grooms on the catwalk. The ceiling consisted of wide open rafters, and the groom would hang upside down from the rafters, by their knees. Then the girls would pull the groom's pants down and rub their bodies against the helpless customer. Initially, Kim said he was not interested. But there were two reasons that Kim would later change his mind. The first reason was the six beers and four shots of tequila that Jeff and I provided him. The second reason was a brief verbal exchange that Kim and I had about a year earlier, during a dispute. The salient part of the conversation went like this:

Me: "Do you know what your problem is?"

Kim: "No, what's my problem?"

Me: "You're a pussy."

Since that incident, Kim had been influenced to do a variety of risky or offensive behaviors, ostensibly to convince me that he was not a pussy. Between the alcohol and his subconscious mind, Kim had lost his free will to make any other decision but to hang from some rafters in public and have his pants pulled down.

By 10:00 p.m. we notified Bambi that Kim would like the smush treatment. She said that would cost $50. Sounded reasonable. Jeff requested *Kashmir* by Led Zepplin to accompany the act. The song captured the reckless spirit of the evening.

Within a few minutes *Kashmir* was blaring throughout *Leave It to Beavers*. Kim was pulled onto the catwalk by three strippers. Then several more strippers joined in, grabbing Kim and rubbing against him. At mid-song, one of the strippers directed Kim to pull himself onto a rafter above the catwalk. Kim hung himself upside down from the rafter by his knees. One of the girls unzipped Kim's pants and pushed the pants up to his knees, exposing his bleached white skivvies. Kim swung unsteadily from the rafter. The crowd of onlookers laughed and catcalled during the spectacle. I turned my head away for a moment and I heard the sound of a body fall on the catwalk. I looked back to see Kim lying on the floor. Jeff abruptly yelled, "He landed right on his head! I think he broke his neck!" I worried about consequences of our actions, including how we would explain Kim's broken neck to Minneray.

For a few dramatic moments Kim crawled around on the stage like a disoriented, wounded, drooling animal. He finally regained some sensibility and we pulled him off the catwalk. We examined him and concluded he was okay, or at least okay enough. We expeditiously took Kim back home then Jeff and I headed back to Motel 6.

The phone rang at Motel 6 at 8 a.m. It was Minneray. She was motivated to call after smelling a strong whiff of alcohol on Kim's breath. "I talked with Kim. I am very unhappy with your behavior last night. However, I am not surprised by your debauchery. But I am disgusted," Minneray said. I told Minneray that Jeff and I were kind of disgusted, with Kim, as well.

We arrived at the wedding site at noon, with a three hour count-down until the wedding. By then Kim was feeling better, but he said his neck was sore and he wasn't sure why. We filled in the sordid details. Kim resolved to show respect for the day as much as possible despite his repugnant behavior the night before.

Kim, Jeff, and I decided to relax in the hot tub which was located near the impending wedding scene. After awhile in the hot tub, Kim said he had a surprise for us. He asked us to follow him to the restroom adjacent to the hot tub. In the bathroom, he pulled out a bag of cocaine. He said this was his way to thank us for making the trip to Wayward for the wedding. I think this was also another ploy to prove that he was not a pussy. We then snorted a couple of lines and headed back to the hot tub to enjoy the euphoria of cocaine combined with warm bubbly water massaging the body as we gazed out upon the Pacific Ocean.

The snorting continued for awhile. After an hour, Stanley, Minneray's husband, approached the hot tub in his bathing suit. He seemed to crave human contact, which was understandable considering he had to share a bedroom with Minneray the night before. Jeff and I urged him to have a beer with us, which he did. After awhile he opened up a bit. He told us about how pleased he was that Hallie was going to marry Kim. He said that he had a rotten marriage, but he still had hope for other people. He felt that Hallie was a kind person and that Kim should not worry about the fact that Hallie's mother was so terrible.

Despite Stanley's good intentions, Kim interpreted Stanley's remarks as a suggestion that Hallie possibly could have inherited the irritating and offensive personality traits of her mother. Kim had never allowed himself to seriously consider this possibility. But the pressure of the advancing wedding combined with Stanley's remarks brought this horrible possibility directly into the center of Kim's consciousness. He was suddenly overwhelmed by a pervasive sense of doom. He felt trapped. Kim then uncharacteristically had a panic attack. He started to breathe heavily and to stutter. He said: "I-I-I don't know if-if-if I can do this. I me-mean-mean get mar-mar-mar-marreeed. What if Hallie ends up being like-like-like Min-Minneray some-someday?" He snorted more cocaine to try to calm down. He referred to Hallie as Minnaray a few times, but corrected himself, which was reassuring.

Then, twenty minutes before the ceremony, a red-faced Minneray rapidly approached the hot tub, wagging her finger and screaming: "What are you doing! You're going to be late for the wedding! Get out of that tub! Now! What's wrong with you!!!"

We obediently got out of the hot tub and went to the staging area to get dressed. Kim was internally and externally disheveled. I wondered if maybe we had taken things a little too far into the gutter.

At 3:00 p.m. I found myself standing next to Kim in front of a makeshift altar on a bluff overlooking the Pacific Ocean. The person officiating the wedding was named Crystal. She was a friend of Hallie's who had a license to marry people in California. She wore a hemp dress printed with smiling blue elephants for the occasion. Crystal opposed the mistreatment of circus elephants, including verbal abuse. She wore this dress in solidarity with her cause.

Hallie was mentally prepping for the traditional walk with her father to the altar, wherein Stanley would symbolically give Hallie away to Kim. Hallie was blissfully unaware of the activities at *Leave It to Beavers* and the cocaine party in the hot tub. She was unaware of her father's public testimony against Minneray in the tub. She was unaware that Kim was grossly ambivalent about getting married to her. She looked as happy as can be.

Crystal extended a warm welcome to the guests gathered on the bluff. She wished Kim and Hallie peace. "I have prayed for the right words to inspire the joining of Kim and Hallie in matrimony," she said. Hallie beamed. Kim turned to me and whispered, "Not sure-sure I can do-do-do this." As is customary for a best man, I reassured Kim that he was doing the right thing and that if he started to hear voices, he should ignore them.

Kim got his gumption up and barely pulled it together. Despite the numbing glaze of alcohol and cocaine lubricating his consciousness, as well as a very sore neck, he was getting through the ceremony. He forgot his cheat sheet with the personalized vows he had written, so he winged it:

"I, Kim-Kim take-take you Hal-Hal-Hallie to be my wed-weddedded wife. I promise to love you and hold-old you despite the prob-prob-problems which happen to about every-everybody. I will make you laugh even though-though you may-may not feel like it. I promise to be your best-best friend. I'm real happy to marrrr-marreee-marry you-you. I mean-mean it. Really."

Hallie was so engrossed with the idea of getting married that she simply smiled and smiled despite Kim's obviously disturbed mental state. Hallie was in la la land.

The ceremony was almost over. Crystal told Kim that he may kiss the bride, three times. But Kim was so preoccupied with a flock of seagulls floating near the bluff, that he was unable to hear Crystal. As Crystal spoke, Kim fantasized that he was a seagull who could simply fly away, *"How beautiful…beautiful…beautiful…beautiful. Why can't I be like them?"* he thought. Finally, Crystal decided she had to end this thing. She quickly pronounced the couple as husband and wife. Then, despite the chaos, Crystal concluded by saying what she always said at the end of weddings: *"I sense that the cosmos supports this marriage."* This was her branding slogan.

The wedding party and guests then moved in unison to the condo clubhouse for the wedding reception. We got some drinks, to celebrate. As anticipated, I was asked to toast the newlyweds. My only regret so far in the festivities was that I had neglected to get a haircut in preparation for my big moment as best man—the toast. Regardless, the toast went something like this:

"I have known Kim and Hallie for several years and I must say that they are wonderful together. As you might have guessed Kim, we have all asked ourselves how Hallie could have possibly chosen to marry you. Our conclusion is that the mystery of human chemistry and the wonders of nature must have conspired to overwhelm Hallie's good judgment. Ahh, isn't nature incredible! But for today, I wish you both long lives, peace, and many beautiful children. I would also like to thank Minneray, Hallie's mother, whom I have had the pleasure to get to know the past couple of days. What a charming woman to have as a mother-in-law Kim. She really is charming! You can certainly see where Hallie gets her personality!"

At that point Kim's face drooped. For a moment I wondered if Kim was having a stroke. He looked pretty bad. I felt a little regret about my sarcasm. Then I gazed over at Minneray, who was smiling as big as day.

Trial by Podium

Creative Consultant:

Susan P. Tyler

I'm not much for taking advice, but there have been exceptions. During my twenties I had little interest in the distant future. Low paying menial jobs met my material needs. I enjoyed school and could have stayed in it forever. After finishing my bachelor's degree in Philosophy, I continued to take undergraduate classes and completed a Psychology major. I planned to complete another undergraduate major in History. I had the benefit of a high quality educational program with the additional benefit of avoiding a serious work life and all of its associated complications. At age twenty-six, I was essentially content.

Then, Indiana University sent me a letter stating that I could no longer take undergraduate classes. They said there were too many of the uneducated waiting, in need of the seat I was sitting in. I concluded that I had some hard choices to make, including, gulp, possibly getting a real job.

So, I had a conversation with my older brother, Terry, about the situation. He said he was aware of my intransigence, and as my older brother, he was obligated to suggest that I get serious about life and consider the future. "If you haven't done anything by age thirty, people start looking at you funny," he said. I was startled by his analysis of my progress as a human being. I thought I was doing pretty well.

After a few days of consideration, I began to think there may be some truth to what my brother said and maybe I should think harder about the future. I began to believe that I needed to do something, and do it fast, to stay on track. The American Dream was at stake. So, I decided that my new goal was to be in a professional position before age thirty.

I considered joining the Navy. I figured the Navy was the safest branch of service. But there was still a possibility of getting killed or seriously injured. For a moment, I considered a corporate job. But I regarded corporate work as a soul killer. Then, I began to wonder about becoming a psychotherapist. My academic background was an excellent fit. Besides that, who wouldn't want to be a psychotherapist? But I needed more information.

So I talked with one of my Psychology professors, Dr. George Heise. He strongly advised me to apply for the three year Ph.D. program in Psychology at Indiana University. Dr. Heise also told me, "Whatever you do, don't go into Social Work. My wife is a social worker. She has spent half of her life dealing with scumbags and tweakers." Dr. Heise was well known and appreciated for his political incorrectness.

Despite Dr. Heise's guidance, I investigated the Master's Degree program in Social Work at the I.U. School of Social Work in Indianapolis. The program had a decent reputation for educating therapists. It was a two year program, so I could finish at age twenty-nine. I decided to head to Indianapolis to pursue my fortune.

I had one concern about the program, however. There were two required areas of study in the program: clinical practice and social policy. The clinical side was appealing. It was simply a training program for becoming a therapist. The policy side was generally regarded as dull by most students however—something to be endured. Those classes involved issues around government entitlements, funding, and related political issues. Not of much interest to me. Frankly, I preferred to sit in therapy classes and talk about ethereal matters.

So, the first semester began. I had five classes including my first policy class, "Social Policy in the Post-World War II Era." The class was taught by a former U.S. Congressman, Horace Bannister. He served two terms in Congress and then retired. As a former congressman, Horace Bannister was accustomed to personal treatment which recognized his status and distinguished background. Anything less than overt bootlicking was inadequate. Horace Bannister was a big shot.

So, the class syllabus consisted of extensive reading and two exams. Additionally, there was a required class presentation on a topic to be agreed upon by Horace Bannister and each student.

I arranged a meeting with Horace Bannister to discuss my presentation topic. I told him that I wanted to research *discrimination of the obese*. Now, Horace Bannister weighed about three-hundred pounds (estimate). I failed to consider that he might be sensitive about this subject. "I don't think you'll be able to find any research on that topic. It is not an issue of concern for serious academics," he said disdainfully. I must have touched a nerve. So, I decided to just go with the flow to avoid further friction.

We continued for another half hour and finally agreed that I would research and discuss "Deficits in Native American Education." This was Horace Bannister's idea. I was uninspired by the subject. No pizzazz. Nevertheless, I thanked Horace Bannister and left. My presentation was scheduled for December 5. I had six long weeks to prepare.

Okay, the campus was crackling with activity approaching December 5. I did my best to procrastinate as long as I could. I even had a fair amount of success at not even *thinking* about the presentation until December 4. By then, I finally grasped how remarkably unprepared I was. I needed to get moving if I was going to come up with something half-way respectable.

So, I found myself at the campus library at 7 p.m. on the evening before the presentation. The library closed at midnight. I had to make hay while I could. I started with a cup of coffee in the student lounge. I noticed a television report that Buckminster Fuller had died. I watched the remainder of his biography. I had another cup of coffee. I balanced my checkbook. Then I noticed it was 8:30 p.m. I had to get to work.

I walked out of the library at midnight with a rough and somewhat incoherent skeleton of a presentation. I felt edgy about the presentation which would take place in only ten hours. But I thought, "This is not the first presentation that I didn't prepare for very well. I'll do okay." I stopped at a Waffle House on the way to my apartment, for a jumbo coffee. I headed home and knocked out a couple more hours of work on the presentation. Then, I collapsed into bed. It took over two hours to get to sleep because of my inadvertent caffeine intoxication.

I woke up late. I had no choice but to drink a large instant coffee, to get myself going. I showed up at the classroom of my Social Policy class at 10 a.m. I tried to problem-solve. I thought, "I might be able to make it through the required twenty minutes, if I talk slower. I bet that would use up two or three minutes." Desperation was setting in.

Horace Bannister stood at the podium preparing for class. He was fumbling around with his papers and superficially chatting with students. He called the class to order. Four students were scheduled to do twenty minute presentations, then up to ten minutes of discussion each.

The first presenter was Angela McKenzie, something of a star in the program. She had worked several years in the field and was admired for her academic skills as well as her magnetic personality. She appeared at the podium and gave a scintillating presentation called *"Commodity Fetishism and its Centrality in Understanding Capitalist Society."* She presented herself gracefully and thoughtfully, as a master of the subject. Fellow students enthusiastically applauded when she finished her presentation.

There were a few questions which Angela McKenzie fielded like a major league all-star shortstop. I was up next.

Horace Bannister called me to the podium. I had bags under my eyes from inadequate sleep. I was long overdue for a haircut, which contributed to my rumpled appearance. I felt jittery from the instant coffee, accompanied by acid indigestion. As I walked to the podium, I suddenly had a piercing yet deep awareness of how unprepared I was. It was like a pessimistic epiphany. The defective quality of my work would soon be laid bare when compared to the artistic magnificence of Angela McKenzie. My sense of doom and self loathing were growing fast.

I took a deep breath and went through my presentation. In general, I can honestly say that it was completely terrible. This was the first time I ever imploded during a public speech. I never stuttered before in my life, nevertheless, I found myself stuttering at times. I sweated profusely, mostly on my face. I completely forgot about talking slower to use up my allotted time. But it wouldn't have helped anyway because I ended up finishing in only eight minutes. Fellow students observing this fiasco mercifully averted their eyes. At the end of the presentation, there was no applause, just silence. I sheepishly took my notes from the podium and returned to my seat.

Horace Bannister approached the podium. For a few long moments, Horace Bannister stared out of a classroom window. He quietly said, "Steve, please come up here for a moment." I came forward and stood next to him in front of the class. He asked if there were any questions. No questions were offered. Then he said:

"Steve, since there are no questions, I would like to discuss what just happened here. You want to be a professional social worker. So you better improve your public speaking skills. It was obvious that you were pathetically unprepared for this presentation. You have humiliated yourself in front of your peers. Following your entrance into the profession, you will

be publicly speaking at times. And you better improve, or else you will not only present yourself as an embarrassment, but the whole profession of Social Work as well!!!"

Okay. I stood there stoically. Then, I slithered back to my seat and watched the next two students do fabulous presentations as I repeatedly replayed in my mind the pitiful show that I had just put on. Finally the class ended. I felt like I became invisible as we all stood up to leave. I moved forward quietly and alone. No one said a word to me. I noticed that they all looked kind of cheerful when the class ended though—as if they were all relieved that what had just happened to me, did not happen to them.

For many years I thought that Horace Bannister had done me a favor by calling me out publicly. This event did in fact make me a better public speaker. I learned my lessons: Prepare well because procrastination can carry a heavy price—and watch the caffeine. After that day, I never even came close to repeating the epic catastrophe of my presentation in Horace Bannister's class. As years passed however, I came to realize that Horace Bannister really did not have to publicly grind on me the way he did. A simple and short conversation in his office would have sufficed.

Finally, anyone who witnessed my self-inflicted disembowelment that day has long forgotten about it. And I no longer wince when I think about the affair. Instead, I simply shake my head in amusement of this event as well as the staggering multitude of other foolishness I have witnessed, and participated in, during my life.

Passenger

Many people have moments in life which are so overwhelmingly powerful that an experience can be remembered in granular detail for the rest of their lives. These moments are often transformative and serve as a basis for a new understanding of themselves and the world.

In February 1981, I was twenty-six years old. I lived in Bloomington, Indiana and worked as a manager at a fast food restaurant. The job primarily involved trying to motivate lazy teenage boys to actually do a little work. I enjoyed the job, but I needed a break. The Grateful Dead would play at the Uptown Theater in Chicago on February 26th. So, I especially appreciated getting the weekend off. I first saw the band five years earlier and immediately fell in love with their music and tried to see them live any chance I could. I planned to attend the concert with Bruce Hill, a former room mate of mine at Indiana University. Bruce was an eccentric guy. A loner. He was a connoisseur of marijuana back in college and had become even more skilled in his ability to obtain and cultivate pot. I anticipated that Bruce's pot expertise would come in handy at the event.

February 26th arrived. I relaxed as I proceeded north on Highway 37 from Bloomington in my 1967 Volkswagen Beetle. As planned, I pulled out a joint and lit it. It was going to be a psychedelic day, and the drive to Chicago was going to be part of it. I felt fabulous about my good fortune.

As I headed north to Chicago, I relaxed into a mild pot induced daze. I took in the barren but beautiful Southern Indiana landscape. I turned on the A.M. radio and found a sermonizing preacher. Despite being agnostic, I have always enjoyed a good sermon. The preacher was in good form that day as he launched into an attack on Secular Humanism. He explained that Secular Humanists believe that humans are *"only animals."* He said that human beings are created in God's image and are consequently much more worthy of God's love. He declared that Secular Humanists are possessed by the devil. He warned against the seduction of the Secular Humanists. The sermon ended and I turned off the radio to digest what I had heard. *"Why do so many religious people hate so much?"* I wondered.

After the sermon, I spotted a hitchhiker and pulled over to give him a ride. (At that time in history, it was customary to be friendly with strangers.) We pulled back on the road and introduced ourselves. His name was Alfred Brundage and he was heading to Chicago. *"Is Brundage a British name?"* I asked. *"I don't recognize nationalities. I am a citizen of human civilization,"* he said. He told me he was named after his uncle who was a bank executive in New York City. *"My uncle is cool, despite being a conformist,"* he said. I appreciated the counter-culture vibe.

Alfred asked me if I wanted to get high. *"Sure."* So we smoked a joint while he explained his reason for going to Chicago. *"I'm going to attend a Native American spirit dance."* Cool.

I could tell that the pot was kicking in when he tangented into the question of the nature of reality. He asked me for my opinion. I gave the stock agnostic answer: *"Who knows?"* Alfred then gave his opinion. He said it was simple, *"Man, it's all one big thing and it just does what it does. That's all you really need to know."* I contemplated Alfred's beatnik wisdom. Then, we both silently went inward and took in the Indiana countryside.

I inserted a cassette tape of the latest Dead album *Terrapin Station* into the tape player. Before long, the song *Passenger* came on. My amped up THC level enabled me to easily associate *Passenger* with the present situation. These lyrics rang true:

Passenger, don't you hear me?

Destination, seen unclearly.

After a couple of hours we were closing in on Chicago. I exited the interstate and pulled over. *"This is where you get off Alfred,"* Alfred Brundage looked at me then got out of the car. He held the door open as he thanked me. His final word was *"Pax."* He shut the door and formed a peace sign with his right hand. I silently wished him a happy spirit dance.

I reached Bruce's apartment and we lit up a joint. Once (again) stoned, we moved in slower motion as we gathered ourselves to go to the Uptown Theater. We hopped in the Beetle and we were there in twenty minutes.

The lavish and beautiful theater was from another era. It was from a time when quality and durability were valued more than functionality and economy. As I pondered stoner thoughts like that, we stood in line to enter. The line moved slowly. As usual, we didn't talk much. Bruce's schizoid personality didn't require a lot of watering.

As I stood in line I noticed a skinny, crazy looking kid walking up and down the line yelling stuff about Jesus. *"Good Lord, give peace a chance,"* I thought. I tried to avoid eye contact, to stay disengaged. I didn't want to participate in any part of the Jesus Freak fanaticism that was afoot in America. This Jesus Freak looked particularly zealous. He circled around and re-approached me. At that point, my judgment lapsed. I inadvertently looked him directly in the eye and BOOM! His eyes locked onto mine and he began to move slowly toward me. There was a slightly tortured look on his barely post-pubescent face. He began carrying on about how the Grateful Dead was possessed by the devil and that I was possessed by the Grateful Dead.

It was unnerving. I avoided eye contact to try to discourage him. It didn't help. Finally, I told him to get lost, which did help. He moved on to find his next lost soul, but the words he had spoken involuntarily echoed in my mind.

Okay. Now, the day was starting to feel a little unusual. This was the second time that day that I heard someone talking about demonic possession. First was the fundamentalist preacher and his message about Secular Humanism. And now a crazy Jesus freak tells me that the Grateful Dead are demon possessed. And, by association, I was possessed as well. I proceeded in the hope that the Jesus freak would be the last unpleasant intrusion into my consciousness for the day. Things would be much better soon...when the music starts.

We entered the Uptown Theater, stricken by its majesty. *"Deadheads have taken over a palace!"* I thought. What was a crowd of misfits doing in a place like this? The theater consisted of ornate features including marble everywhere, huge columns, heavy velvet drapes, and elegant brass appointments. There were two stairways arcing from the lobby to the balcony. Stained glass windows separated the upper level vestibule from the auditorium. The scene possibly could have been lifted from one of Edgar Allen Poe's opium dreams. And it was gloriously intimate. The theater seated only 4,500 people. Perfect.

Our seats were located in the middle of the balcony close to the railing, giving us a spectacular view of the stage. As usual, we did some people watching for a few minutes. There is a lot of different humanity on display at Dead concerts. The variety ranged from broke-down hipsters to college professors. The one thing they all shared in common was their fascination with the Grateful Dead.

As with all Grateful Dead concerts, there was a shared belief that something incredible and possibly inexplicable was soon going to happen. The band performed feats of wonder. They created a musical environment where the mind roams. The mood and meaning of the music changed dramatically and you changed too. Sometimes the music was euphoric. Sometimes it was poignantly sad. Under all circumstances, the music triggered memories, emotions, and ideas.

The Grateful Dead is a secular/musical religion. And as in most religions, Dead World is steeped in imagery and symbolism in the form of logos, posters, and album covers. That night, the stage was adorned with a large Steal Your Face logo located behind the band. It is the most well known Dead logo and it is particularly provocative. It looks like this:

The band members casually walked on-stage and were enthusiastically greeted by cheers from the audience. As the band tuned up, Bruce and I completed our concert preparation. Grateful Dead concerts are wrought with rituals, including the one involving smoking a joint at the appearance of the band. I handed Bruce a joint and he lit it up.

Ahhh, the aroma of great weed! We passed the joint back and forth several times until the guy next to me asked for a hit. Then he handed it to someone else, and then it disappeared. Within a couple of minutes we were feeling the familiar euphoria. No chatting with Bruce, so I surveyed the scene and contemplated the ensuing bacchanal.

The Dead sometimes take the first two or three songs essentially to warm up. But not that night. They came out red hot, opening with *Feel Like a Stranger.* This is one of the band's few overtly sexual songs. A great opener. We might as well get the animal spirits going. The crowd roared it's approval. In an interlude about three minutes in came the lyrics: *"Gonna be a long long, crazy crazy night."* I didn't realize how prescient these words were at the time.

Next came *Althea*, a very dark song seemingly about love lost via narcissism. The song is like a Rorschach test. And like a Rorschach test, songs can elicit truth. As I listened to *Althea*, I reflected back on past foolishness and misjudgments which had hurt others. I figured that most of the crowd was taking a similar trip down their own shady corner of memory lane:

Can't talk to you without talking to me.

We're guilty of the same old thing.

Thinking a lot about less and less.

And forgetting the love we bring.

We were only about twenty minutes into the concert when *Althea* ended. Then came *Little Red Rooster*. This is a blues number made famous by The Rolling Stones. Not quite my favorite choice. *"Why does the Dead play non-Dead music? What's the point?"* I thought. Bruce tapped my shoulder and asked if I wanted to smoke another joint. We needed to think strategically. It seemed a little soon to light up again. On the other hand, it made sense to smoke another one during *Red Rooster* to avoid distraction later. Bruce pulled a joint out of his jacket. It looked like this:

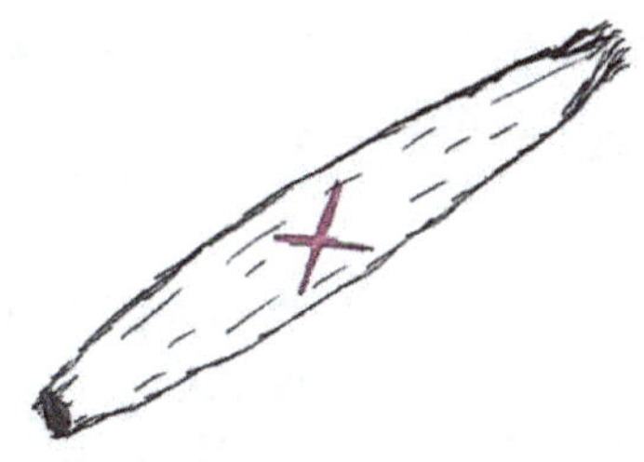

"What's with the red X?" I asked.

"It's special," Bruce said. He smiled widely.

"What's special about it?"

"Higher grade," Bruce replied.

Made sense to me. *"Okay."*

The music was too loud for me to hear my inner voice whispering a quiet but earnest request for caution. Recklessness was taking over. Out came the Bic lighter. We ignited the special joint and finished smoking it as *Rooster* plodded along. And...things began to change.

Bird Song was next. Another song about love and it's inevitable loss. My mind automatically traveled to the wasteland of my history with girls (as I called them back then). Despite romantic travails, I think I did the best I could with what I had at the time. Hey, from what I have seen, I think all of us always do the best we can with what we've got. We have no choice.

I looked over at Bruce. He was wearing sunglasses now. We were drifting apart, as if we were on two separate ice floes succumbing to different currents. But I didn't care. My mind was occupied by the music.

Then came *Me & My Uncle* and *Big River* in rowdy, rapid succession. The music began to take on a pounding, aggressive feeling. The theater was illuminated in rich tones of red, white, and blue lights. It felt like a baptism, by sound and light. In *Big River*, I heard growling in Bob Weir's voice. Jerry Garcia's guitar was communicating messages in a different language--a language without words.

Peggy-O was next. I felt relieved that the mood was shifting to the mellow euphoria of *Peggy-O*. This is a ballad about a man who becomes a soldier to gain status, to marry his beloved. In the end he is killed and buried a thousand miles away. Despite his best intentions, his dream was not meant to be. The crowd was quiet, pensive. As if in a holy place. The song ended gently and peacefully, in contrast to what was coming next.

The band then detonated into *Passenger*. In a split second, the room was engulfed in a maelstrom. The band played furiously, with a single mind. Every person in the theater was on their feet and moving. I looked down and viewed the audience on the ground floor. The crowd had their arms raised, palms open toward the band, as if in a salute. Their bodies moved like windblown stalks of wheat waving in unison. Ecstasy was breaking out! The stage looked like an altar. Except, instead of a cross above the band, there was this:

Passenger's message exploded like a psychological atomic bomb:

What is a man

Deep down inside

But a raging beast

With nothing to hide!

The crowd roared, ferociously but joyfully! And I had an epiphany. It was as if a lightening bolt had penetrated my mind, and revealed the meaning of the strange occurrences I witnessed that day: the hateful sermon on Secular Humanism, the hip hitch-hiker, and the fanatic Jesus Freak. These experiences had prepared me for this moment. Passenger's Secular Humanistic message ripped into my consciousness. Then, the normal boundaries of my mind shattered and the true nature of the universe became clear:

People who believe in God think that God rules the universe like an emperor. They believe that like an emperor, God thinks, feels, and makes judgments.

But actually, the universe is more like a plant. It simply grows according to it's nature.

And incredibly, at that moment I believed that the ultimate purpose of the universe was to reveal its nature, TO ME! Now that I understood one simple idea--that the universe is like a plant, the purpose of the universe was fulfilled. And just like a plant whose purpose is fulfilled, the universe would now cease to exist. The universe was about to vanish!

I knew another truth: I needed to get out of there. I was overwhelmed by fireballs of sound and terrifying teleological thoughts which had invaded my consciousness. I was certain that the universe was about to disappear. It would soon cease to exist as instantaneously and magically as it had come into existence. I was terrified that not only me, but everything I had ever loved was about to be gone forever. I arose out of my seat and aimed myself rapidly toward the back of the theater. I headed toward the safest space available to me. The men's room.

I soon found myself in front of the mirror in the men's room. It felt like a miracle to see my own face in the mirror. As I looked at my reflection, I heard my mother's voice telling me that I needed a haircut. She was probably right. A few guys passed through the men's room, but they weren't particularly interested in the existential crisis I was having. Seeing people freak out is not really all that unusual at Dead concerts. These guys just wanted to take a leak and quickly get back to the music. Regardless, I calmed myself as much as possible. After about ten minutes, I decided to head back.

I came out of the men's room and approached the wall of stained glass windows separating the vestibule from the auditorium. The vestibule reverberated from the pounding force of the music. Fantastic colored light streamed through the stained glass. As I opened the door and looked into the auditorium, white beams of light flowed into my eyes. What I saw looked like the interior of a nuclear reactor. I had to back away from the door a couple of times before I had the gumption to re-enter.

I moved down the aisle and approached my empty seat, and Bruce. He was still wearing his sunglasses. He looked addled, if not downright deranged. Bruce slowly turned his head toward me and yelled, *"You alright?"* I paused and yelled back, *"Sure. Fine. Never better."*

The rest of that concert is a blur. For awhile, I ruminated on the notion that the universe might vanish. But before the music stopped, I realized that I had simply succumbed to a cloud of delusion.

However, my view of the world changed that day. Since then, I have embraced the simple yet enlightening idea that the universe is like a plant-- a single magical plant that consists of all things big and small. A plant that is simply fulfilling its nature. When translated into beatnik language, this notion can be succinctly expressed as: *Man, it's all one big thing and it just does what it does. That's all you really need to know.*

Raising Riley

Creative Consultant:

Susan P. Tyler

Hi. My name is Molly Tyler. And for your information, I'm a dog. I've been a member of the Tyler pack now for thirteen years. Like any other journey, this journey has been wrought with ups and downs. But for me, raising Riley was the darkest period of my life.

Before I get into telling you about this dark period, I will tell you about my idyllic life before Riley. I was found at the Humane Society by my pack leaders, Susan and Steve Tyler. I was given to their son Jack, as a birthday present. Spending my early years as a companion to a sweet little human boy from ages twelve to eighteen was any dog's dream. It was like being in a warm cocoon of love and affection, without a worry. Then Jack went off to college and I was left with Steve and Susan, which was okay despite a few minor adjustments. Steve was easy to train. That guy will give you about anything you want, if you just bat an eye at him. Susan is another story however. Tough as nails.

The other contender in the home was Maggie, my predecessor. Maggie was like a sweet and dear older sister to me. Never an unkind growl, only the cajoling kind of growl. I imagined that someday I could be a warm loving figure to a younger dog, with Maggie by my side to coach me. But that dream was not meant to be. Maggie passed away when I was six years old.

So Jack came home for a visit from college. One day during his visit, he took some girl to the Humane Society to look at dogs and they discovered a little black and white puppy named Riley. They thought she was adorable. Jack even said she was a "Sugardog," a reference to Sugar, the legendary first Tyler family dog who had a black and white coat as well. Man, I've spent half of my life hearing how wonderful Sugar was. I mean really, no one is that perfect! As a dog, I try not to not carry resentments. But the Sugar issue is really a trigger for me.

Jack noticed that Riley was energetic and playful. What Jack did not notice was that she was caged alone, which indicated that she was not suitable to be around other dogs. She was also housed in a restricted area, as if there might be radioactive material in there somewhere.

Nobody noticed that Riley was a lunatic. She jumped up and down continuously. It was like she was riding a souped up electric powered pogo stick. I hear that Sugar was energetic as a puppy as well. But when she was taken outside to play, she calmed down like a normal dog and she attended to things like sweet smelling flowers or other creatures. But, as we all found out later, Riley was wired very differently. It seemed like she was in her own world—a world of aggression and disregard for the simplest rules. I worried that she was a sociopath, which is an unusual diagnosis for a dog. But in this case, it seemed to apply. (By the way, Steve used to be a social worker and his psychobabble and diagnosing habit rubbed off on me. Sorry.)

Well Jack took Steve to the Humane Society to check out Riley. "She's a lot like Sugar," Steve told Jack. Yeah, yeah, yeah. Well, Steve and Jack conspired to convince Susan that adopting Riley was a great idea. Their approach was manipulative, but it worked.

Jack and Steve told Susan about Riley and suggested that she simply go look at her at the Humane Society. They knew that Susan could not resist the smell of puppy breath or the soft feel of puppy fur. They didn't have to ask her to adopt the dog. It was game over once she got within ten feet of Riley. Unfortunately, Jack and Steve were right about Susan's weakness for puppies. Susan, no all of us, were drawn into the trap of owning a monster.

Well, they brought Riley home, unsuspecting what was to come. Everyone knows puppies are a lot of work, but Riley was in extreme need of training. To be fair, she was pretty easily house trained. But she had a rampant disregard for property and seemed motivated to destroy all types of things.

We also noticed that Riley had a compulsive need to bite ankles and feet. Steve would say: "She must have a herding instinct." That's ridiculous. She just wanted to hurt people and she was so short that the only spots she could reach were ankles and feet.

One thing I noticed that the humans missed: Riley did not wag her tail when we got her at age three months. Most dogs are wagging within a few days of birth. Tail wagging is a dog's way to let other dogs know their mood, and their intentions. The absence of wagging was further evidence that something was amiss with Riley.

We soon noticed that objects in the home were being systematically destroyed. One of Riley's first projects was stripping the leather off of a couch. The couch was soon taped up with red duct tape. Even as a dog, I found this kind of trashy. Riley chewed up Steve's cell phone cover, which he never replaced due to his pervasive sense of pessimism and doom during this time. Steve estimated that Riley destroyed about $3,000 worth of stuff around the house. Man, that could have bought us a ton of Milk Bones.

Consequently, the house turned into what looked like a high security prison. Each room had a gate to limit Riley's movements in the house. This made moving around the house complicated. I did enjoy being separated from Riley for much of the day however. When we were together, it was an unending stream of puppy attacks. Mostly feet biting.

As you know, some puppies need to sleep in a crate for a few days, maybe a couple of weeks. But Riley slept in a crate for months. At bedtime, there was a routine battle to get Riley into the crate. Then she would bounce around in it, knocking it noisily against the wall. The scene could have been taken from *The Exorcist*, minus the green vomit. It kind of shook us up right before sleep time—which led to nightmares for the three sane ones sharing the room with Riley.

Going for walks was a "psychedelic experience," as Steve likes to say. Riley would forcefully and inexorably pull on the leash. Susan became concerned that Riley might damage her trachea. So they got her a "gentle leader," which is a strap wrapped around her snout to avoid stressing the trachea. This was planned to be a temporary arrangement. However, Riley pulls forcefully on the gentle leader too. So it looks like she will never get back to using a regular collar. She always makes things so difficult for herself.

Riley's behavior was so bad that Steve and Susan took her for dog training at a SmartPet store. I heard Susan and Steve talk about this a lot. Now the trainer, Ernie, was terrible. But that was irrelevant. The other dogs seemed to do okay despite Ernie. The only thing Riley learned in her formal education was how to shake hands. That's it. Big deal.

This problem with Riley affected not just Susan, Steve, and me. It also affected our sweet coon hound cousin Daisy Tyler who lives in Elyria, Ohio. Daisy not only heard about Riley's mania, but she witnessed it first hand when Daisy visited. She could hardly bear to hear of Riley's insane and undoglike behavior. In despair, she frequently howled and worried about Riley. It was terrible.

Susan and Steve speculated about what to do with Riley. Dog training school was no help. The conventional methods used with previous dogs were useless. One evening Steve brought up the incomprehensible. He suggested that Riley be RETURNED to the Humane Society. But Susan stood strong: "I think someday Riley is going to be a great dog," she said. Steve respected Susan's opinions. But he was still pessimistic.

I was shocked to hear the "RETURN" word come out of Steve's mouth. As a former tenant of the Humane Society, I couldn't allow this to happen. I decided that I had to take over the training. Susan and Steve are decent people, but they don't understand dogs. Pups like this need constant reminders of what is expected, and what is intolerable. I began closely observing Riley and giving her "feedback" when she misbehaved. That's a polite way of saying I humped and pinned her regularly. She seemed to enjoy this moment of domination, as if she felt more like a real dog and not some phony miniature human being.

Over a four month period, I was on that mutt on a regular basis. Twice I pinned her against a couch holding her by the throat with my teeth, which sent her a very clear message. And when I wasn't on her, I was benignly neglecting her (to use one of Steve's phrases). And lo and behold, when she turned one year old, she was as docile as a piece of cherry pie.

Time has passed. Our home and pack are at peace again. At the dog park recently some reckless mutt came running toward Riley and I automatically came to her aid and diverted the other dog. I thought about how things have changed and my growing attachment to Riley. I'm glad we didn't give up on her. She's a happy, tail wagging dog now. It's been a long road, but great things are worth waiting for.

The Buffkin House

Creative Consultant: Susan P. Tyler

My wife Susan and I intended to send our first born child, Joe, to kindergarten at Harcourt School. Like most parents, we were anxious about sending our little boy out into the world without our protection.

The school invited parents to attend an *"Ice Cream Social"* to meet teachers and get oriented to the school about one week before school started. We met Mrs. Schmidt, our assigned kindergarten teacher. We had a brief but life altering conversation with her. She stated: *"I've been teaching for over thirty years now. And I'll tell you, when I get to the point I just can't take it anymore, I'll just quit! I mean it. I'll just walk out!"* We were alarmed. Susan and I decided, even before we left the ice cream social, that we could not send Joe into a classroom with this lunatic teacher. The fact that she was already wigged out before school even started was a bad sign. We believed our only option was to move to another school district to enable us to send Joe to another, more desirable school--a school without Mrs. Schmidt.

Spring Mill School was the closest school available. And it had a great reputation. Susan and I met with the principal, Nancy Locklander. Mrs. Locklander was sympathetic and agreed to make an exception to enroll Joe. But she asked that we agree to move into the Spring Mill district as soon as possible to be in compliance with school administration rules.

The real-estate market was active and there were only a small number of houses in our price range available in the Spring Mill School district. We narrowed our search to three homes. The first two had obvious disqualifying problems. But the third house seemed interesting. The home was owned by the Buffkin family.

Gladys Buffkin, the lady of the house, told us she had a realtor's license and would be handling the sale herself. The house had been on the market for over one year and the price had just been reduced by $41,000! It was a large ranch style home, four bedrooms, two and a half baths, fireplace, basement, and my favorite: a hot tub in the back yard.

Our initial impression of the house was extremely positive. Susan was pleased with the layout of the home and the fact that it was on a dead end street--a great safety feature for kids. I was impressed by the hot tub. I immediately imagined how much fun Susan and I could have in the back yard in that thing. We told Mrs. Buffkin that we would like to have some family members come back to look over the house and she agreed to meet the following day at five o'clock.

We arrived at the appointed time the following day with Susan's parents as well as Janine Hubertson, our realtor. Mrs. Buffkin told us that some other people had requested to see the house and asked if this was okay with us. Despite feeling somewhat irritated by the change of plan, we agreed.

As we toured the house, we noticed that there were indeed two women also viewing the place. As I passed the two in the living room, one said: *"This place is fantastic, I bet it won't be on the market very long! And the price has been reduced by $41,000. Unbelievable!"* I wondered if these two ladies might be shills. After some reflection, I concluded that it was unlikely that Mrs. Buffkin would or could be that manipulative.

Mrs. Buffkin took Susan and me outside to show us the grounds. In the front yard we noticed a drainage ditch which was filled with water from the house's sump pump. This despite no rain the previous few days. There were two ducks swimming in the ditch. *"This ditch looks like it might be a problem,"* I said. Mrs. Buffkin responded quickly: *"It is so nice to have water in the yard. It's like a water feature! These ducks make this their home. They come back every year. It is really quite wonderful!"* I was charmed by the ducks and responded: *"Yeah, I guess it would be nice to have ducks in the yard."*

From the front yard I noticed that the gable atop one of the front bedrooms sagged. This was disconcerting. *"That gable looks like it is sagging. That looks like a problem to me."* I said. Gladys Buffkin responded:

"I don't see anything. Maybe that's an optical illusion. No one's ever said that before." My denial system kicked in and we moved on.

We toured the inside of the house. In the basement, I noticed that the house had two sump pump pits. I had never seen two pits in one house before. *"Why are there two sump pits?"* I asked. *"That is just a security feature. You can bet that a lot of people would sleep better at night with two sump pits."* Gladys Buffkin said. *"That makes sense,"* I thought.

At the end of the tour, I told Gladys Buffkin that we liked the house but it was still above our price range, despite the price reduction. She replied: *"As a real estate agent I think I can help you with that. In the real-estate world, we encourage young buyers to spend a little bit more than they are comfortable with. Your family will grow over time and you'll be glad you have a bigger house. In the long run you'll save money by not having to move to a bigger house someday. It all makes sense when you consider the future growth of your family."* Made sense to me. I temporarily forgot that I had a vasectomy a few months earlier, and consequently, the family presumably wouldn't be growing.

At home that night, Susan and I discussed pros and cons. Susan was convinced that this house was right for us. My biggest reservation at that time was the roof. *"I get a bad vibe from that roof. Someday we'll want to sell that thing and I wonder how many people will walk away from a saggy roof."* Susan thought I was making a big deal of the roof, so I let it go.

It didn't take long to make a decision. We invited Janine Hubertson over to discuss an offer. By this time, my ambivalence was completely mitigated and I was ready to buy this fabulous house, with a hot tub! Janine Hubertson was also excited about our decision. *"Now we just have to come up with a dollar offer. I must tell you though, I talked with Gladys Buffkin this afternoon and she says someone would like to make a cash offer, so if you want this house, we better get an offer in quickly,"* she said.

"Do you think that's for real?" I asked.

"As a licensed realtor, she is forbidden from lying about something like that." Janine Hubertson said.

After some brief consideration, my grandiosity kicked in. I said: *"Let's just offer them the asking price! That's a really nice house and I think the Buffkin's deserve a decent price. No reason to quibble."*

"Sounds great to me!" Janine Hubertson said. *"I'll get the offer to the Buffkins tonight!"*

Janine Hubertson submitted the offer to the Buffkins. They immediately accepted. I was a little concerned because there was apparently no cash offer to slow down the negotiation. We forged ahead anyway. A move in date was established. We had one month to prepare our old house for sale and to make room in our hearts for a new home.

The intervening month was a very busy time. We did some minor upgrades in our existing house and it sold quickly. We had lived in that little place for seven years, never had a problem with it. We spent hours cleaning the house and it was immaculate. Before we walked out the door to our new life, Susan and I placed a bottle of Cabernet in the fridge for the new owners. We wanted them to be happy.

We arrived at the Buffkin house in an Avis truck and with a variety of family members to help. This was going to be a triumphant day! One of the greatest days of our lives! My fantasy had the day ending with Susan and I having a glass of champagne in the hot tub! I approached the front door of the Buffkin house and rang the doorbell. After a couple of minutes, Gladys Buffkin opened the door. She said hello and paused. I said, *"Mrs. Buffkin, we're here to move in."*

"Today's not a good day. I think we'll have to reschedule and do this tomorrow, or maybe sometime next week," she said.

"What?" I said.

"Today's not a good day for us. We have most of the big stuff out, but we have a ton of smaller things. This is going to take us awhile."

"That's unfortunate, but we have a contract stating we move in, right now. We have moved out of our house and all of our belongings are in that truck," I said as I pointed at the moving van.

"Okay. Give us a couple of hours and we'll be ready," she said.

"No, we'll give you fifteen minutes, then we will start to move this stuff into the house."

Mrs. Buffkin slammed the door shut. I was stunned at the audacity of these people. But there wasn't time to dawdle. We began staging belongings from the truck in the yard to get things moving. About twenty minutes later the front door opened and the process began to proceed. It was a hot day but there was a cold chill in the air as we quietly passed the Buffkins moving out as we moved in.

Our family was so helpful. I felt obligated to work harder than anyone involved in the undertaking. But we began to run into problems. First, our dog, Sugar, was stressed and confused and getting in the way. I grabbed her collar in order to pull her into the back yard. She turned and bit two of my fingers and the thumb on my right hand. This left me with a cut and bleeding hand. It was a sweltering and sweaty day and bandages would not stick on the wounds. I wondered if I should get a tetanus shot and maybe some stitches. But I didn't have the time for a trip to the emergency room. I was able to locate some rubber gloves and put one on my right hand to keep from bleeding on our stuff.

I worked furiously throughout the day to get the many tasks done which were necessary to get everyone in bed that night. I put together the bunk beds, the baby's crib, filled our waterbed. And with every task there was some sort of intervening obstacle. I gave up on the dream of Susan and me in the hot tub with a bottle of Champaign.

As a consequence of the heat and sweat on moving day, I got a case of jock rash that could have rivaled any jock rash ever had by Attila the Hun. I could barely sleep that night for the burning pain. The deep dog bite on my hand ached. The first night in the house I also got a spider bite on my neck while sleeping. The bite was right near my Adams apple and was swollen red for a few days. I later learned the house was full of wolf spiders.

The Buffkins had gone out of their way to leave the house filthy. Besides that, they left a lot of big stuff in the house with the promise that they would come get it the next weekend. This included an old rusty refrigerator, big filing cabinets, and two large broken down wooden bookshelves in the basement. Well, they never came back. But they did manage to lure the neighbors across the street into volunteering to take the stuff.

My new neighbor, Bill Klawitter, showed up and looked at the stuff, which was junk, of course. Out of a sense of neighborliness, Bill offered to take it away. I ended up helping him haul this stuff up the basement stairs and across the street. I wondered how it happened that I was doing the Buffkin's heavy lifting.

My new neighbors had a lot to say about our new house, and the Buffkins. Tom Donopolis, the Buffkin's neighbor for 25 years, introduced himself. He then launched into a monologue about how sleazy and swindling the Buffkins were. *"You could sue them, because somehow or other they must have cheated you,"* he said. Another neighbor, Mr. Sanford, introduced himself this way: *"Hi, I'm Joel Sanford. Well, you are probably finding out about all of the things wrong with the Buffkin house."* He told me about how Gladys Buffkin had called him after we made our offer and asked him to lie about the flooding problems in the area if, by chance, we had an opportunity to talk with him.

A week after we moved in, we had a new septic system installed in the front yard, as planned. This was paid for by the Buffkins as part of the deal. They hired a guy named John Adams to do the job. John Adams obliterated our front yard with his backhoe. For about two weeks, there were huge mountains of dirt in the front yard. After that, for weeks, there was mud and septic plumbing debris everywhere as the grass began to sprout.

When the septic system was completed, John Adams pulled me over and said: *"You better hope this system works, because there ain't no place left on your property to put another one."* I wondered: *"Why did we ever buy a house with a septic system anyway?"* John Adams advised us to call a septic tank company to have the tank pumped out. *"The contents of that tank are mostly solid. It ain't been emptied in years. No time to waste or you might be in the market for a new septic tank."*

So I called the *Indy Sewage Pumping Company*. I described the problem to one of the workers. I gave the address of our new home and he said: *"Oh, you mean the old Buffkin House?"* *"Yesss,"* I said. They came out and removed the big turd. *"That's one of the worst poop balls we ever seen. We charge an extra fifty dollars for a job like this."*

I began work clearing a lot of the weeds and debris left in the back yard. I got into some poison ivy. It started out small, on my forearms. It began to spread slowly for two days. On the third day I woke up and found it all over my chest and abdomen as well. I went to our doctor to get treatment for the poison ivy. I thought: *"Everything will be all right if I can just get rid of this poison ivy."* The doctor prescribed an extra long course of Prednisone due to severity of the rash. *"We don't want to mess around with a severe case like this,"* he said.

I became obsessed with growing the grass in the front yard. I spent hours picking up debris. I was concerned about the kids possibly being exposed to ancient poop which adhered to the broken tiles now scattered about the yard. I also became aware that giant crows were eating the grass seed early in the morning. One day the Prednisone woke me up at 5:00 a.m. I spotted a group of giant crows gobbling on the grass seed. I got a BB gun and snuck around to the corner of the house, in my underwear, and started shooting at the crows. Susan later said, *"What if the neighbors would have seen you?"* I responded: *"I don't care."*

I set my sights on the hot tub. It appeared that the Buffkin's dog, Woody, had been bathed in the tub witnessed by a mass of white fur floating on top of the water. I drained and cleaned the tub. Woody had also shed about five tons of white fur in between the slats of wood on the deck. I spent an afternoon out there scraping out dog fur. I also scraped a sizable hole into my right index finger doing this task. This was the same hand that was healing from Sugar's dog bite.

We decided to have a party to celebrate the new house and to thank our family for helping with the move. The party was gearing up and I began to muse: *"This is a great house!"* Then I heard my mother-in-law's voice: *"Steve, Steve, come here!"* She pulled me into the spare bathroom and pointed at the overflowing toilet. It was flowing not only in the bathroom but under the hallway and down the driveway. My plumber brother-in-law could not explain the problem. We found out the next day that the septic guys had cut the line from that toilet leading to the septic system. The pipe from the toilet was running right into the ground.

The Prednisone made me noticeably more irritable than usual. One night, Susan, a nurse, got home from work a little late, after midnight. I began to get hostile about it, suggesting she was flirting with the young physicians at the hospital, etc, etc. Now, this is really out of character for me. In addition, Susan noticed that I was getting a little strange about the electrical appliances. I refused to plug in the electric air cleaner in the boy's room one night. She asked me why and I said: *"It's electrical. It might catch fire if we plug it in."* Susan paused for a moment. *"I think you're paranoid,"* she said. Her remark was not particularly concerning because Susan frequently tells me I'm paranoid.

I felt amazingly strong and powerful on the Prednisone. For several days as I drove home from work, I found myself listening to *The Doors*. I played the song, *Riders on the Storm* on my car cassette player over and over. Jim Morrison seemed to have a special message directed only at me. The Prednisone made me an even more aggressive driver too. I recall flipping off a few other drivers on my ride home from work if they pissed me off.

We decided to have the roof reinforced due to the sagging gable. We hired Jim Kabuta, a contractor who did that job as well as a few other minor repairs. He completed the job. *"How much?"* I asked. *"Six hundred and sixty dollars,"* he said. My facial expression revealed my discouragement.

"What's wrong," he asked.

"I'm just tired of laying out cash to get this place livable," I said.

"Can I give you some advice?" he said.

"Sure," I responded.

"It's only money," he said.

"What do you mean by that?" I said.

It looks like you have healthy kids and a pretty wife. You can always get more money, but you already have what is really important," he said. I hadn't thought of it that way.

A few days later, Susan sent me to the Lazarus department store. I saw Gladys Buffkin in the store with the same two women we had seen at the house viewing. Gladys Buffkin averted her eyes when she noticed me in the store. Normally, I would have sucked it up, but the Prednisone instructed me to confront her directly.

I approached Gladys Buffkin and said: *"I see you brought your shills out for some shopping. I suppose you're out spending some of the cash that you swindled from us."*

"I don't know what you're talking about. Please leave or I will call the police," she said.

"I bet the cops know all about you. Just so you know, I have contacted an attorney and I plan to sue you," I said. I had not really contacted a lawyer, but she didn't know that.

"Just leave us alone you moron," she said.

"See you in court Buffkin," I said.

I walked out of the store. I was pissed. I got into my car and turned on *Riders on the Storm*, to soothe my nerves. Jim Morrison sang it silky smooth: *"There's a killer on the road, his brain is squirmin' like a toad. If you give this man a ride sweet family will die, etc, etc, etc."* The vibe helped to mellow me out following the ugly confrontation with Gladys Buffkin.

I returned home. Susan was at the front door and looked distressed. *"I was using the kitchen sink and the water just kept backing up, so I called Roto Rooter,"* Susan said. A couple of hours later it was determined that the kitchen sink was also not connected to the septic system. I called Jake Melancamp, the plumber who failed to connect the sink to the septic system.

He came out the next day and repaired the problem. *"If you have any other plumbing issues call me up and I'll do the work for free to make up for this."* I had a faucet problem about two weeks later and called Jake Melancamp. It sounded like he was in a bar. *"I have a faucet problem. I would like your help. Remember you said you would do some work to make up for the kitchen sink problem?"* He responded: *"I think you just want a free plumber."* Then he hung up. *"Just another day in the Buffkin house,"* I thought. Then I blurted out a raft of profanity which shocked even Susan who had heard me cuss thousands of times, but never like that.

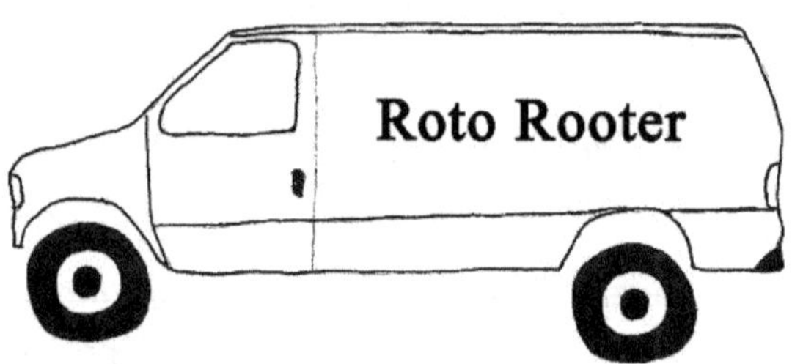

Over time, the storm passed. I completed the course of Prednisone and I returned to my normal level of paranoia and irritability. The house began to heal. We got used to having a lot of unexpected debt. We began to feel comfortable calling the house *our home.*

A couple of years later our neighbor, Bill Klawitter, moved his family to a new house. He returned to the neighborhood a few weeks later. He told me that his new house had tremendous problems and he was unexpectedly laying out a ton of dough. He looked demoralized. I asked if I could give him some advice and he agreed. I told him: *"Bill, its only money."* Bill responded: *"What do you mean by that?"*

Dangerous Curves Ahead

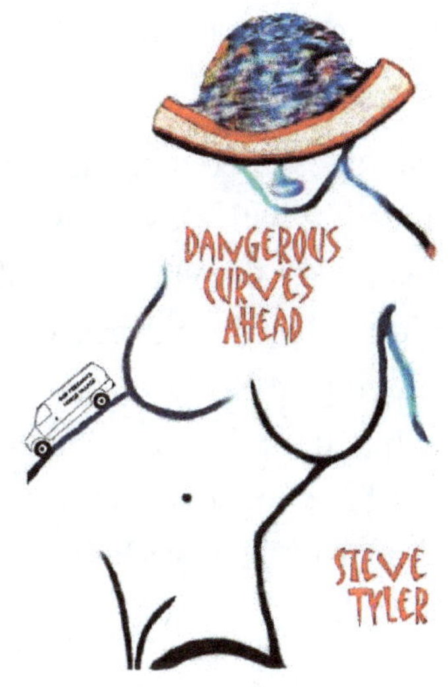

The first time Alexander Berkely called Passages Center, he hung up when the receptionist answered. He just couldn't pull the trigger. He had never engaged in psychotherapy before. He never considered that he needed that kind of help. But at age twenty-two, Alex was confronted with some hard choices. After completing a Bachelor's Degree from Indiana University as a Philosophy major, Alex felt like he had awoken from a beautiful dream and found himself on the precipice of the dreary and obligated world of adult life. Alex had been committed to learning the ideas of the great minds in history. Consequently, Alex found himself struggling to find a way to feed and clothe himself following his graduation. Alex had been told, by almost everyone observing his college career, that there would be a day of reckoning. That day had now arrived.

The telephone call to Passages, a counseling center, was preceded two weeks earlier by a chance meeting with David Moss, a long time friend and school-mate. Alex ran into David at the university library. They had a brief but memorable conversation. David told Alex he had completed his business degree and was moving to St. Louis to work as an accountant at Generique, a plastics manufacturer. He planned to marry his girlfriend, Vicki, in about a year. "All I have left to do is get a new wardrobe for the job." David said. A quotation from Henry David Thoreau flashed through Alex's mind: "*Beware of all enterprises that require new clothes.*"

David's plan represented a sad but not unusual lack of imagination to Alex. Alex's friend embraced the American Dream: college, marriage to the college sweetheart, corporate job, mortgage, and babies soon to follow. Alex believed that people locked themselves into cages in pursuit of this alleged dream. He considered this vision of life a recipe for regret culminating in a mid-life crisis--a lack of purpose. The crisis most likely ends in divorce followed by the purchase of the proverbial red convertible.

The following weekend, Alex was confronted again with the same issue. Alex and his apartment-mate, Christopher McGowan, met one evening and split a six pack at a local limestone quarry to discuss the post-college problem. Chris told Alex that he planned to move back home, to Atlanta, Georgia. His plan was to get a job and marry his girlfriend, Marilyn. "Alex, we both have some important decisions to make. There are some dangerous curves ahead, my friend. There could be long term consequences if we slip up now."

"You're right, these are big decisions Chris. But look at what Bloomington has to offer. There's a new flock of beautiful girls bussed in every September. The quarries. The ridiculously low cost of living. And I.U. is the locus of the fairly limited amount of intelligence and culture in Indiana. Why would anyone leave paradise for a meat grinder like Atlanta, Georgia? Why?"

"Man, it's time to move on. Your problem is that you're a hedonist. Even your interest in Philosophy is hedonistic. You're in love with brain-candy! It's time to leave Disneyland. It's time to grow up and start suffering like everyone else!"

Despite his disdain for the American Dream, Alex was having trouble maintaining his conviction about how to proceed after college. Alex's friends appeared to be gleefully surrendering to the allure of conformity. Consequently, Alex began to question himself. He was unemployed and low on cash. He needed a neutral party to help him sort things out. He considered trying some counseling. If nothing else, he figured it might at least be interesting.

The second time Alex called Passages, he did not hang up. The receptionist answered and Alex arranged an appointment with a therapist. Her name was Beverly Thornton. She was a fairly newly minted psychologist, about five years out of graduate school. Alex scheduled to see her in one week.

In the meantime, Alex continued to look for work. Given his pathetic financial situation, he was open to about anything. He looked at the Help

Wanted section of the *Bloomington Reporter* and found an advertisement for a job as a laundry delivery driver. Alex called Bob Freeman, the owner of Bob Freeman's Norge Village, to inquire about the job. Mr. Freeman asked Alex to come in immediately to talk. The previous driver had quit a few days earlier and Bob was highly motivated to fill the position.

Alex drove over to the laundromat which displayed an unusually large sign which read *"Bob Freeman's Norge Village."* There was a new dark blue 1977 Cadillac parked in front of a sign which read *"Reserved for Bob Freeman."* Alex went in and found Bob Freeman talking to the two employees who processed the laundry, Alma and Glenda. They were a mother and daughter team who had been with Bob for a few years. Bob gave Alex a brief tour of the Norge Village. Then Bob and Alex went to Bob's office to discuss business.

Bob quickly got to the point. He offered Alex two dollars an hour to serve as the delivery driver. Alex noticed an unusually large diamond ring on Bob's right hand ring finger. Given the Cadillac and the over-sized diamond, it looked like Bob could certainly afford a more reasonable amount. "Mr. Freeman, I'm really interested in the job, but I need at least one-hundred dollars a week just to maintain myself." Bob paused then replied, "Well, that's okay, if that's what you need." "That was easy," Alex thought. Alex accepted the job and agreed to start the following day.

Bob got down to specifics, "Now, our answering service is a lady named Mrs. Harris. She will contact you every morning to give you addresses of customers wanting pick-up. Alma and Glenda will have those pick-ups done the next day for delivery." Bob gave Alex the keys to a white 1971 Econoline van. The laundry van looked like this:

The next morning at nine o'clock, promptly, Alex's phone rang. It was Mrs. Harris, the "answering service." In reality, Mrs. Harris was on Disability and Bob paid her in cash to help support her. Her only activity was answering the phone for Bob. She was available all day and night for a laundry call. "Did Bob tell you I am hard of hearing? If you can speak up when we talk that would make things a lot easier for me." "I understand," Alex said.

Mrs. Harris was very chatty and interested in Alex's story. When he told Mrs. Harris he had just graduated from college she asked: "If you just graduated from college, why are you delivering laundry?" Alex told her it was his life's dream and she laughed.

The day of Alex's first therapy appointment arrived. He made it over to Passages for a three o'clock appointment. He checked in with the receptionist who gave him a stack of papers to fill out. Alex dutifully completed the forms.

Beverly Thornton opened the door to the waiting room ten minutes late. Alex was slightly irritated by her tardiness, but his irritation quickly dissipated after he got a look at Dr. Thornton. She was a stunning brunette in a rather tight fitting red and black dress. Alex was pleasantly surprised. She was certainly not what he expected. Alex regretted not getting a haircut before the appointment.

Beverly Thornton approached him, "Alex?" "Yes," he said. "Come with me please." Alex eagerly followed his new therapist to her office. He sat down on a cushy couch and momentarily mused at the notion of being on a couch in a therapist's office. He wondered if it was okay to lay down. Dr. Thornton sat down in her swivel chair and introduced herself: "I'm Beverly Thornton. I'm a psychologist here at Passages. You are scheduled for an evaluation today. Thank you for doing the intake paperwork. Please give me a moment to look it over and then we can start."

"That's fine." Alex was now free to surveil the office environment. There were two diplomas and a license on one wall which conferred a sense of authority and achievement. The room had five well groomed plants and some generic landscape pictures on the walls. He looked to see if she might have a picture of a boyfriend or husband on display. Nope. Alex looked at her left ring finger. No ring. "Hmmm." he thought. Beverly finished with the paperwork. "Alex, now I would like you to tell me what brings you to therapy."

"Of course. I'm having a hard time deciding what's next. I just graduated from I.U. with a Philosophy degree. And as you might suspect, it is rather difficult to find employers looking for people whose greatest asset is an above average understanding of Epistemology and Existentialism. And I see my friends moving on, like robots, to pursue conventional lives. I want to find my own way. But I'm lacking in direction."

"You want to avoid a life of quiet desperation."

"Well, yes. So you're a Thoreau fan. How refreshing," Alex said.

"Thoreau had a lot to say about how to live. It sounds like our goal for therapy will be to resolve your ambivalence and get you on your own road to the future. Have you found any means to support yourself until you find your path forward?"

"Yes, I just got a job delivering laundry. Not too glamorous, but it will keep me afloat." Beverly responded, "Sometimes jobs like that can be surprisingly interesting." "We'll see," Alex said.

After the session, Alex reflected on the experience. Alex found Beverly Thornton intriguing. It wasn't just her good looks that fascinated him. He found her reference to Henry David Thoreau as attractive as her remarkable curves.

Over the next few weeks, Alex became familiar with the routine of his new job. He developed a fondness for Mrs. Harris. He began to look forward to her morning calls. "Did I wake you up?" "Yep." "You're a grown man. You should be up and about by nine o'clock!"

It became apparent as well that Mrs. Harris had trouble accurately obtaining addresses of new customers. Due to her poor hearing, she would sometimes transpose address numbers or give incorrect street names.

One time, it took Alex four attempts to find the home of a customer who lived about ten miles outside of Bloomington. Alex spent hours driving through the countryside looking for non-existent addresses until the day Mrs. Harris finally gave him the accurate one. The new customer was named Don Pendleton. As Alex drove up the winding driveway to his home, Mr. Pendleton was driving his red Lincoln Continental down the driveway toward him. They approached each other, stopped, and got out of their vehicles.

"Are you from the laundry service?"

"Yeah."

"Man, what took you so long? I've been calling for two weeks."

"Our answering service lady is kind of deaf, sorry. She has a hard time getting addresses right."

"Hmmm. A deaf answering service lady. That sounds like a problem that could be solved."

"The boss is trying to help her out."

"Well, in any case, our well went dry, so we are in a bind. We're just about out of clean clothes. I was just leaving to go to a laundromat to do this stuff myself."

The Lincoln was full of bags of laundry--front seat, back seat, trunk. Full. Alex transferred the laundry to the van. "I'll make sure you get this back tomorrow. Sorry for the inconvenience."

Alex returned to the Norge Village, excited about the big catch. "Hey Bob, you won't believe what I picked up this morning. We struck the motherload!" Bob surveyed the massive pile of clothes in the back of the van. "This is the largest order we've ever brought in!" Bob declared. Alex cut to the chase: "This guy is loaded Bob."

Alma and Glenda went to work and had the order completed the following day. As Alex loaded up for delivery, he asked Bob how much he was going to charge. Bob paused to consider. "One-hundred and fifty dollars," he said. Despite the size of the order, the price seemed outrageous, even to Alex.

Alex returned to the Pendleton estate for delivery. Mr. Pendleton was pleased to get his delivery and readily wrote a check for one-hundred and fifty dollars. Alex agreed to return the following week for another pick-up.

Don Pendleton had about half the laundry for the second week pickup. Alex asked Bob what the charge would be and he replied, "One-hundred and fifty dollars." Alex delivered the load and informed Mr. Pendleton of the price. Pendleton shrugged and said, "Alright." He wrote a check.

The following week, another load from Mr. Pendleton. That load was about one-third the size of the first order. Alex asked Bob, "How much?" Bob replied, "One-hundred and fifty dollars." "You're the boss!" Alex replied. "Man, Bob's got some balls," Alex thought.

Upon delivery, Don Pendleton questioned the price. "Is it one-hundred and fifty dollars no matter how much laundry?" "I'll talk to Bob," Alex said.

After a discussion with Bob, a decision was made to charge forty dollars per week, no matter the size of the load. Don Pendleton felt like he was getting a great deal, although he really wasn't. This is called "The Door in the Face Technique." Bob was amused that this maneuver actually had a name.

Many of Alex's customers were well off financially. Some were just plain poor. One day Alex saw a two dollar charge going out. Alex thought the charge should have been closer to ten dollars. He asked Bob if there was a mistake on the billing ticket. "No. That's the Armstrong's order. They can't afford a washing machine and they can't afford to pay us any more than that. I've offered to do it for free, but they won't let me." Glenda was standing nearby and said, "Bob's like the Robin Hood of laundry!"

About half of the customers paid on delivery, but some put their bill on a tab. Bob's wife, Betty, did the billing for those customers. She mailed bills out once per year. "Sending bills is such a hassle. It's a lot easier to do it just once a year. And we save a lot on stamps!" she told Alex. On one occasion, a customer received her annual bill and had a tantrum when she confronted Alex about this. "How does Bob expect me to pay $350 for laundry? This is crazy!"

Alex discussed the problem with Bob and he paused and said, "Oh, let's just let it go. She's a nice lady. And she used to baby-sit our kids." So, weekly service to this lady continued and she kept running up her bill.

Bob would defy conventional laws of commerce in other ways as well. Alex was instructed to obtain gasoline for the laundry van at *Gary's Pro Station*. The gasoline charges went on Bob's account. Months later, Gary, the gas station owner, approached Alex and said: "Hey, could you tell Bob that I would appreciate it if he would pay his bill. It's almost Christmas and I would like to buy my kids some presents." Alex relayed the message to Bob.

After a few weeks, Bob still had not made a payment. "That's just how Bob is," Gary told Alex. Eventually, Bob and Gary completed their ritualized little dance and Bob finally, reluctantly, coughed up the money. Alex discovered that in rural Southern Indiana, economics was not simply a function of business. It was based on friendship as well. People were generally kind and patient with each other. At times, it felt like the normal laws of economics simply did not apply.

In therapy, Alex became comfortable and opened up to Beverly Thornton. This primarily involved discussions of Alex's early life as well as his goals for the future. He told Beverly:

> *"My father toiled all of his life, starting with service in World War II, followed by a wife and four kids. He spent decades running his own business. He had a heart attack at age fifty-two. He died six days later. During those last few days he told me that when he was sixteen years old he spent a summer in Hannibal, Missouri to help build a YMCA. The rest of his life, he dreamed of spending a summer rafting down the Mississippi River. But this dream was not meant to be. His life was consumed by multiple unrelenting responsibilities. He told me that not fulfilling this dream was his only regret and he urged me not to make the same mistake."*

"So, that is what you mean when you say people create cages for themselves?" Beverly replied.

"Yes. My goal is to be free. I don't want to be encumbered by work, relationships, or other commitments. I want to be free to experience life on my own terms."

"Alex, it takes courage to swim against the currents of society. But I'm guessing that your father found deep satisfaction in building his life and honoring his commitments. It sounds like overall, despite his one regret, he lived the life he wanted."

Alex paused and reflected. "I think you're right Beverly," Alex said. This simple clarification enabled Alex to consider the importance of commitment in achieving a good life.

One day at the Norge Village, Bob mentioned that he was a pilot and that he had a Cessna single prop airplane. He asked Alex if he would like to go up with him sometime. Alex enthusiastically agreed and a couple of days later Alex found himself 10,000 feet above Southern Indiana. First, Bob flew over the laundromat and circled it three times. "There it is, our mother's milk, ha ha ha!" Then Bob flew over nearby Lake Monroe. As the two passed over the center of the lake, Bob said: "You're not going to believe this, but this plane can do an almost ninety degree climb without the wings falling off! Watch this!" Bob abruptly pulled back on the control wheel and the plane shot nearly straight upward. "Ha ha ha ha, isn't this great!" Bob yelled.

The enjoyment Bob showed in about everything he did was contagious. Alex asked him: "What's your secret Bob? You are an expert at living!"

Bob paused for a moment to think. "When I was a boy, my grandpa told me: 'Life is like an empty canvas. It's up to us to paint the prettiest picture we can.' That's what I try to do, I try to paint a pretty picture."

"That's a wonderfully simple way of looking at life." Alex said.

"Simple is good!" Bob replied.

After about an hour in the air, Bob said, "It's time to head back. On the way, I have something to talk with you about."

"What's on your mind?" Alex asked.

"Well, I have a business proposition for you. I'm going to retire in about five years. I think it would be great if you could take over the business then. We could create an arrangement where you buy me out, over time. I can tell you enjoy the work. And you have good business instincts. I can understand this possibility may not be what you planned after college, but I would be really pleased to hand the business over to you."

"Bob, this is quite a surprise. I appreciate the offer. I just need a little time to think about it."

"That's fine. Take your time." Bob replied

A couple of days later, Alex had an appointment with Beverly Thornton. He wanted to talk with her about Bob's proposition as well as another issue. Beverly greeted Alex in the waiting room and they walked back to her office.

"How are you Alex?" she asked.

"Doing great, thanks Beverly. I have some interesting news. I had a conversation with Bob Freeman. He plans to retire in about five years and he has offered to sell me the business."

"You sound enthusiastic. Have you made a decision yet?"

"Yes. I'm going to do it."

"What is your thinking on this Alex?" Beverly asked.

"What I can tell you is that the past ten months have been the most satisfying of my life. I enjoy the work, the people. And most importantly, I feel like a free man, not a glorified indentured servant! I accidentally fell into what I've been seeking but didn't realize it until two days ago."

"Sometimes the world brings us what we need, whether we know it or not." Beverly said.

"I'm beginning to believe that," Alex said. "Beverly, there is something else I would like to talk about."

"Yes, Alex."

"Beverly, I would like to get to know you better, outside of this office, I mean."

Beverly responded cautiously. "I appreciate that Alex. But I have to abide by a professional code of ethics. In my profession it is not ethical to have a personal relationship with patients."

"Is there some way to work around that problem?"

"You're putting me in a difficult situation," said Beverly.

"The bottom line is that we are ultimately just two human beings. We could have just as easily met at a cafe or a grocery store. We just happened to meet this way. Now, there must be some way to work around this."

"Well the code of ethics does say that social relationships are acceptable if there is no contact for six months following treatment."

"So, if I quit therapy and call you in six months, what happens?"

"I don't know. That six month rule is there for a reason. It gives both parties a chance to contemplate that possibility. I would have to wait and see how I feel then."

"I'll take a chance on that."

So the session ended cordially but not as satisfying as Alex had hoped. As agreed he ended his contact with Beverly Thornton and focused his energy on developing a working plan with Bob Freeman. In five years, Alex assumed ownership of the laundromat. The name was changed to *Alex Berkely's Norge Village*.

*****

At age twenty-eight, Alex attended his ten year high school reunion. He was impressed with how much his classmates had changed, yet stayed the same. As Alex made his way through the crowd, he ran into his old friend, David Moss. He greeted David and they proceeded to update each other.

"The last time I saw you was in Bloomington at the library. You were preparing to move to St. Louis to work as an accountant. And I remember that you said you were going to marry your girlfriend, Vickie."

"How can you remember that? That was so long ago," David said.

"You just made an impression on me that day, David. That's all. How did St. Louis work out for you?"

"I'm still working at Generique. But it's a grind."

"What about Vickie?" Alex asked.

"We got divorced. It only lasted about three years. We went into a spiral and just couldn't recover. You know, it's a not an unusual story. So, what have you been up to?"

"I'm still living in Bloomington, and I still love it there. I bought and run a laundromat. It's a simple but good life."

"A laundromat. Hmmm."

Just then a beautiful brunette approached the two men and stood next to Alex. "Hi. Here's your drink, sweetie." She handed Alex a gin and tonic.

"David, I would like you to meet my wife, Beverly. Beverly, this is David Moss."

"Nice to meet you, Beverly," David said.

"Nice to meet you too, David. I've heard a lot about you."

Cafeteria Kerfuffle

Creative Consultant: Susan P. Tyler

I felt unusually optimistic as I rode down the escalator to the cafeteria located in the basement of the Indiana University library. I was there to meet the cafeteria manager for a job interview for a dishwashing position. It was my third year at Indiana University and I needed cash. Pent up anticipation for the freedom to run my own life fueled impetuous spending during the prior two years. Now it was time to pay dues and replenish the bank account.

I entered the cafeteria and asked a staff member for Lucille Rafalko, the cafeteria manager. The staff member introduced himself. "I'm Mitchell Fisk. Hey, I bet you're here for a job interview. I'll let Mrs. Rafalko know you are here. Oh, by the way, this is a cool place to work." Mitchell Fisk disappeared behind the counter area and then into a nearby office. He summoned Lucille Rafalko.

Lucille Rafalko was a cheerful, if not jovial, sixty year old woman. She smiled broadly then reached out her hand and introduced herself. "Hello, I'm Lucille Rafalko. You must be Steve. I'm so glad you called about the job."

"It's nice to meet you Mrs. Rafalko." I said.

"Please call me Lucy."

"Well thank you Lucy. Wow, I love the name 'Rafalko!'" It is like a mouthful of crunchy consonants mingled with a few friendly vowels."

Mrs. Rafalko giggled girlishly, "My goodness, no one has ever commented on my name like that before. I'll have to remember that one. Come into my office and we can chat," she said.

I followed Lucy Rafalko into her office. We discussed the role of the job, work hours, expectations. "It's nice to be nice," she said. "That's the official motto of the cafeteria. I expect customers and staff to be treated courteously and respectfully. And, of course, the work must be properly done." Mrs. Rafalko had a kind spirit, unlike some of the jerk bosses that I had worked for. We arranged a schedule. I would start in two days.

My first shift at the cafeteria started at 4 p.m. and lasted until midnight. I discovered that the cafeteria was quiet and studious during the day, but assumed the ambience of a large, caffeine fueled party after dusk.

Mrs. Rafalko rarely appeared in the evenings. She zoomed out the door at 4 p.m. After she left, the cafeteria was handled by the assistant manager, a guy named Dennis. No one seemed to know his last name or anything much about him. He was an expert at hiding his whereabouts, which worked just fine for the staff.

There were usually two staff members assigned to the dishes. My dish washing partner that night was Aaron Cohen. Aaron was an intellectual character, seemingly out of place within the confines of the dish room. "Welcome to heaven," he said enthusiastically. "I'm Aaron, good to meet you. This place is glorious. I think you'll like it."

"What makes this place so wonderful?" I asked.

"Lucy," Aaron responded.

Within a short period of time, I found myself enjoying the job more than I expected. I wasn't getting rich, but I was having a good time. Part of the pleasure was Mrs. Rafalko. She was considerate and charming—simply a genuine person. In fact, she had me over to her place a couple of times for a gin and tonic. We were unexpectedly becoming friends.

Well, my work situation was apparently too enjoyable for the work gods to tolerate. I arrived at 6 p.m. one evening and I was surprised to see Mrs. Rafalko still in her office. She asked me to come in and shut the door.

"An order has come down from administration. They tell me that all staff with beards have to shave or be terminated. They think beard hair could possibly contaminate cafeteria food. I wanted to discuss this in person with you boys. The deadline is in one month.

"You're kidding," I said.

"Unfortunately not. I know you boys might have feelings about the situation. I hope we can work together to deal with this problem."

"Well, I guess the administration doesn't ascribe to our motto: 'It's nice to be nice,' because this is not very nice."

"Can I speak in confidence?

"Of course," I said.

"I agree with you Steve. I have tried to influence admin to drop the plan, but they seem determined to make it happen."

"Hey Lucy, I believe you. I know you wouldn't support something like this. It's offensive. I need some time to think about it all," I said.

I headed back to the kitchen. I could see discomfort on Aaron and Mitchell's bearded faces. Like someone was squeezing their nuts. I knew the feeling. We decided to take a break to discuss the matter.

"This sucks. I guess the big people must have nothing better to do than worry about our grooming habits," Aaron said.

Mitchell chimed in. "This is outrageous. I'm not shaving! And you know what, I think this is illegal. This rule will affect only males. This is sexual discrimination!"

"Well I'll just schedule some time with my attorney and make a plan to take on Indiana University in court. No problem," I said.

"Hey man, this is 1976. There is something called the Human Rights Commission in Bloomington. We can file a sexual discrimination complaint against I.U. I don't think an attorney is required," Mitchell said.

Aaron capitulated. "I'm just going to shave it off. I don't have time for this nonsense."

"I'm in for a fight," Mitchell declared.

"Let's quietly talk with the other guys. Don't tell Lucy though. I don't want to upset her. I'll get some information about the Human Rights Commission to find out what is possible," I said.

I visited the Bloomington Human Rights Commission office and discussed the problem with Alvin Corker, an advisor there. He explained that the Commission could see this case in a couple weeks, once the paperwork was submitted. "Do I need an attorney?" I asked. "No. If you've seen Perry Mason a couple of times you can handle it," he said.

I arranged to have a few interested male staff members get together to discuss a possible action against I.U. They generally felt that the cause was hopeless. They believed I.U. was just too powerful to defeat. Mitchell Fisk was present. Despite earlier saying he wanted to fight, he now declined to get involved. "Too busy." If a sexual discrimination complaint was going to happen, I was going to have to do it myself.

A hearing took place two weeks later in a meeting room at the Bloomington City County building. Indiana University had two attorneys present. The lead attorney was Raphael Torrez. Before the hearing he told me that four attorneys were working on the case. "I.U. is concerned. They don't like to have their authority challenged," he told me. "I agree. I.U. also has a habit of unnecessarily intruding into people's private business. Which is why we are here today," I replied. Torrez sneered and said: "Good luck, you're gonna need it."

The commissioners were headed by Chairwoman Lois Baumgartner. The commission had two other members: Dr. Richard Johnson and Reverend Brianna Loudermilk. Ms. Baumgartner called the meeting to order. She said, "The complainant will present the complaint, then the university will respond. We understand that the university has a witness. This witness may testify after Mr. Torrez rebuts the complaint. Mr. Tyler, you may begin."

"I want to thank the commission for hearing this complaint. I am a student worker at the I.U. Library Cafeteria, which is part of I.U. Food Services. Indiana University Food Services has arbitrarily instituted a rule that staff cannot have facial hair. This takes effect in two weeks. Apparently the university believes they have the right to infringe on the personal liberty of their staff, with the questionable claim that beard hair is a health hazard. The Library Cafeteria staff has not been informed of any illness or contagion emanating from any I.U. food service. This may lead one to believe that this action is whimsical as well as oblivious to the simple freedom of I.U. Food Service employees to groom themselves as they see fit. This action also constitutes sexual discrimination, due to the fact that this rule will adversely affect only male staff."

"Mr. Torrez. You may present the university's position," Ms. Baumgartner stated.

"Thank you Chairwoman Baumgartner. Indiana University takes the position that the creation of the facial hair rule is within their rights as an employer and otherwise satisfies the Human Rights ordinance in Monroe County. The university has the right and duty to protect consumers at their food service outlets. The decision was not 'whimsical,' as Mr. Tyler just

suggested. This issue was researched by our health director and is not an unusual expectation. Many restaurants have such a rule. Our health director is here today and he can provide further information about the new rule and the reasoning behind it."

Charles Minett, the Director of Health at the university took the stand. "I have been employed at the university for seventeen years. I am in charge of monitoring the health environment to minimize the risk of disease. I was involved in the decision regarding the beard rule. The scientific basis of the rule is that facial hair carries bacteria. Facial hair frequently sheds and can contaminate food, causing disease,"

Charles Minett pulled out a Petri dish and displayed it to the commissioners. "This Petri dish has had a sample of a beard hair in it for the past forty-eight hours. As you can see, there is a ring of bacteria growing around the hair. Our goal is to have the safest environment we can for the benefit of our customers. This is not possible when food is exposed to facial hair."

"Mr. Tyler, do you have any questions for Mr. Minett?" Asked Chairwoman Baumgartner. "Yes I do," I said.

"Mr. Minett, thank you for your statement. I found it very interesting. I have a couple of questions. First, how much education do you have in the health area?"

"Most of my learning has been on the job. We get a lot of in-service trainings which have been very informative," he said.

"How much formal education have you had?" I asked.

"High school," he said quietly.

"I see. I have completed two college level biology classes, which means that I have more college level education in these matters than you do. Doesn't it?" I asked.

"Ms. Baumgartner, I object!" Blurted Torrez. Mr. Tyler's educational background is not relevant!"

"The question is rhetorical," Lois Baumgartner said. "You don't have to answer Mr. Minett. Mr. Tyler, you seem to have skill at frustrating Mr. Torrez. Please continue."

"Thank you Chairwoman Baumgartner. Mr. Minett, do you know what percentage of all bacteria is harmful?" I asked.

"No," he said.

"Five percent. In fact, most bacteria are either beneficial or harmless to humans. The bacteria in that Petri dish have only a five percent chance of harming anyone," I said.

"Thank you Mr. Minett. I have no more questions for you. Chairwoman Baumgartener, would it be appropriate for me to ask Mr. Torrez a question? This is regarding a factual claim he made in his rebuttal statement."

"That would be acceptable," she said.

"I object Chairwoman Baumgartner. I am legal counsel representing Indiana University. I cannot be called as a witness," Torrez said.

"We are playing by the rules of the Human Rights Commission, Mr. Torrez. Anyone in this proceeding can be questioned about claims of fact. Go ahead Mr. Tyler."

"Mr. Torrez, you said that many restaurants have a rule limiting beards around food. Can you give me an estimate of how many restaurants in Monroe County have such a rule?"

"I don't have an actual number," he said."

"How many restaurants in just Bloomington have such a rule?" I asked.

"I don't know," he said.

"Can you name one restaurant in Bloomington that has such a rule?" I asked.

Torrez paused, then sighed, "No I can't," he said.

"Those are all the questions that I have Chairwoman Baumgartner. Thank you," I said.

After a bit more haggling with Mr. Torrez, Lois Baumgartner stated that the commission would temporarily adjourn to make a decision about how to proceed. After fifteen minutes, they returned. Lois Baumgartner read the decision: *"By a vote of two to one, it is the decision of the Human Rights Commission to issue a temporary injunction against Indiana University to prevent the introduction of the beard rule for two weeks. In addition, the injunction will require that Mr. Tyler cannot be terminated from the Library Cafeteria for any reason during the period of the injunction. We will reconvene in two weeks to announce a final decision about a possible permanent injunction."*

As I left the hearing, Mr. Torrez approached me. "You got lucky," he said. I responded: "Four attorneys working on this case and you came up with this farce? You better be careful or good ol' I.U. might make some new rules for you too. Like one that says you are no longer employed."

At my next work shift, I was greeted as a conquering hero. I received many high fives and a couple of hugs from the ladies. I could hardly believe it myself—an injunction against I.U. It felt like this was turning into a

David and Goliath story. Unfortunately, I began to show symptoms of an inflamed hubris.

Don Potter, a reporter at the *Indiana Daily Student* newspaper contacted me. He requested that we meet to discuss the human rights complaint. We met at the Brigantine bar. We made some small talk at first and discovered some shared interests. In particular, we were both involved with the socialist party on campus. This created the illusion of a bond between us. I began to feel like Don Potter was my friend. Don Potter was my comrade.

As a consequence of beer combined with the sheer ecstasy of a temporary injunction against I.U., my brain told me to be completely open and express myself. Which I did. This included the following remarks: *"There are people there [cafeteria] with more hair on their arms than I have on my face."* I referred to my job as *"a minimum wage menial job."* And, in regard to my own beard: *"It's not like a disposable thing, it's like my fucking arm."* Of course, my new best friend, Don Potter, wrote an article exactly quoting these words of wisdom in the *Indiana Daily Student*. Hey, no hard feelings. Don Potter was just doing his job.

Now this created problems for me. My next shift at work I spoke with Lucy Rafalko. She was upset. "I saw the article in the IDS. I want you to know that it hurt my feelings when you said you had a menial job. Some staff that have worked here for years, including me, believe that this work is important. Hospitality and serving others is not menial. Otherwise, I really don't know why you had to make such a huge kerfuffle over all this."

"I don't know either. I guess I just don't like being told what to do," I said. "I apologize for hurting your feelings. That was not my intention." Lucy coyly smiled indicating she accepted my apology.

Well, I did some reconnaissance. A few days before the next hearing, I went to visit Alvin Corker at the Human Rights Commission. I asked him if he had heard anything about the case. He said, "I saw the article in the IDS. That was some good stuff. I did hear Lois Baumgartner discussing your case with Dick Johnson. They were both pretty disgusted with the article. I think the 'F bomb' might be a game changer."

"Oooh wow. Well, thanks for giving me a heads up." I said.

The next hearing came and went quickly. The Human Rights Commission simply reported out that a final vote was taken. The vote was two to one against any further action. The complaint was dismissed. Indiana University was now free to fire me.

The day following the hearing, I appeared for what I suspected would be my last day of work at the Library Cafeteria. I prepared for work by shaving off my beard. Lucy Rafalko was waiting for me. She met me as I entered the cafeteria. "We need to talk," she said. Her face was uncharacteristically tense and blushed. I knew what was coming.

"I've got to tell you that you're terminated. Orders from on high. Not my choice." She said. "I can't believe you shaved your beard. Did you think that would make a difference now?" She asked.

"Oh no, not at all. I'm just demonstrating that I'm a free man." I said.

"You're so dramatic," Lucy Rafalko observed. Lucy quickly seemed calmer just getting things off her chest. Although she had just fired me, within a few minutes she invited me over for a gin and tonic the next weekend.

I had unwittingly transformed myself from conquering hero to drama queen within a few days. Hubris and a potty mouth had ended my crusade. But things continued to happen.

A couple of days later I got a call from Fred Breeden, manager of the I.U. grounds crew. He and the grounds crew staff had followed the beard case in the *Indiana Daily Student*. The crew was a band of bearded rednecks who felt I had been screwed over by the university. As beard lovers, they kind of took it personally. So, sight unseen, Fred Breeden offered me a job. Better pay as well. Just like that, I was on the Indiana University payroll again. Ahhhhhh.

As planned, I followed through with gin and tonic in the company of Lucille Rafalko. This was enjoyable. We laughed about the recent kerfuffle and other nonsense. One of the last things she said to me was especially memorable: "You look pretty good shaved. But I think it's about time for a haircut." Lucille was unforgettable, in a wonderful kind of way.

This story is dedicated to my mother,

Ardell Lucille Tyler

Before the writing began:

Theme: Pick your battles carefully

Mitchell Fisk

Laura Fisk

Lucille Rafalko

Luis Torrez

Aaron Cohen

Young men needing a cause

Catching waves

Possible Characters

Alex Berkely

Bob Freeman

Jeff Hill

Beverly Thornton

Horace Bannister

If the cafeteria model is to expect customers and staff to be treated courteously and respectfully. Shouldn't that standard be applicable to the university at large?

Overconfident after first hearing.

END: Oh, I've been meaning to tell you. I think you could use a haircut.

On the Road with Wally

Creative Consultant: Kenneth W. Teeter

Spiritual Advisor: Susan P. Tyler

It was the summer of 1975. A telephone call interrupted what seemed to be just another bleak week in South Bend, Indiana. My mother was fatigued by the presence of my twenty year old unemployed face constantly around the house. The situation was wearing on us both.

The phone rang. It was my cousin Kenny Teeter in Louisville inviting me on an adventure: "A friend of my parents is going to his daughter's wedding in L.A. He needs some help with the driving," Kenny Said. "Get down to Louisville by six and we go to Los Angeles for free." I borrowed a hundred bucks from my mother. She smiled as she handed me five $20 bills. I packed up a few items then headed to Louisville. As I pulled out of the driveway, my mother yelled, "Maybe you can get your hair cut in California after you get there."

I arrived in Louisville, greeted by Kenny and his parents. Within minutes, Wally showed up. Wally Kneedirt was in his mid-forties, friendly, but edgy. "We got to get moving. We're already behind schedule," Wally said. We quickly threw our stuff in the back of Wally's Ford Country Squire wagon. Kenny needed some sleep. He nestled in the back of the Country Squire.

We headed west out of Louisville. Kenny was snoozing and Wally and I were left to get to know each other.

"What kind of work do you do?" Wally asked.

"I'm a student at I.U. What about you?" I said.

"I'm a professional salesman. Right now I'm selling memberships at a wholesale club. It's called '*Cardinal Consumer*.' They use cardinals on their logo. You know, cardinals are the state bird of Kentucky. Pretty clever advertising, huh? The Cardinal is a solid place to work. Hey, they don't know it, but the Cardinal is paying for this trip, ha ha."

"What do you mean?" I said.

"The trip will be on my expense account. I told them I wanted to go to a conference in L.A. and they agreed to pay for the whole thing. One of the gals at the Cardinal is going to make up some phony receipts. Reimbursement for gasoline will be at least $700. Then there's food and hotels. And then there's the big kahuna, the fake registration fee of $900. God bless the Cardinal."

"How long you worked at the Cardinal?" I asked.

"About a month," Wally said.

"That's pretty ballsy after working there for only a month. You worry about getting caught?"

"No, I've done this at lots of places I worked. It's amazing how much people will trust someone they hardly know," he said.

I heard Kenny stirring in the back of the wagon. "How you doing?" I asked.

"Oh, I'm okay. I think I might have to take a leak," Kenny said.

Wally broke in, "Okay. I just want to let you know that we aren't stopping to pee every five minutes. So get the job done when you can. I'm not going to risk being late for the wedding. You understand?"

"Yes sir," Kenny said. "Can we stop and get something to eat?" One of Wally's favorite restaurants, *Frijoles Y Arroz* appeared at the next interchange.

"I'll pull in here and we can get some carry-out. We can save time that way," Wally said.

Wally had two gigantic bean burritos. He quickly snarfed them down, He gathered his empty paper bag, empty root beer bottle, food wrappings, and napkins. Then he pitched it all out of the passenger window onto the road at 80 miles per hour.

I looked at Wally and said, "I guess you're a litter bug."

"What do you mean by that?" Wally said.

"You never heard of Lady Bird Johnson?"

"Oh I get it. You think I was littering. You better suck it up Jack . Or else someday you'll grow up to make somebody a real nice grandmother," Wally said.

A few minutes down the road, Wally blurted out: "That's a New Hampshire plate. I bet they come down in the summer to fish in the gulf. That's a long way to go to fish."

A few minutes later: "There's one from Ohio. I've never been there. I hear it's nice."

A few minutes later: "There's a Florida plate. I wonder what they are doing in Missouri."

A few minutes later: "Hey, there's one all the way from Maine. Can you believe that?"

"Are you going to do this all across the country?" I asked.

"Hey, it's my car. And it's a free country. I have a right to talk about anything I want. You probably don't agree with that. Most of you college boys are just baby Sandinistas." Wally said.

"Hmmm," I said.

It took only six hours for open hostility to break out. It was just a matter of time. Wally was remarkably annoying. I decided that I wouldn't let Wally get under my skin. I needed to preserve my energy and good vibes for L.A.

Kenny and I slept most of the night. Wally refused to let us do any driving. He wanted to see if he could do all of the driving by himself. At 3 a.m. we stopped at a Waffle House. The place reeked of stale coffee, cigarettes, and dirty feet. Kenny and I ate quickly then went out back by the trash dumpster to get some fresh air and discuss our situation.

"How do you put up with that guy? I said.

"I know he's an idiot, but you get used to him after awhile," Kenny said.

"Is he a friend of yours?" I said.

"My parents met him at a Howard Johnson's. They discovered that Wally lives about four blocks from us. He just keeps coming around. He drops in about once a week, around dinner time, for a free meal. My parents have just tried to be polite." Kenny said.

"I try not to hold being an idiot against people. You know, they can't really help it." Kenny said.

"Well he's smart enough to be ripping off Cardinal Consumer for the cost of this trip. He told me he is making fake receipts to submit for reimbursement." I said.

"Lots of people do stuff like that. He's a powerless guy who is just trying to even things up a little bit." Kenny said.

"That's an enlightening way to look at theft, Kenny. You sound like John Dillinger." I said.

We left the Waffle House and got back on the road. We were running about three hours outside of Phoenix. Wally was at the wheel and about to fall asleep. Wally repeatedly slapped his own face to stay awake. We begged him to let us drive. "I can do it myself," Wally yelled hysterically. "We have to make it to Phoenix tonight!!!" Kenny and I took turns yelling at Wally to keep him awake.

We pulled into a rest stop. Wally fell unconscious quickly and we moved him to the back of the Country Squire. We could finally relax with Wally out of the picture for awhile.

"We need to let Wally know that we aren't going to let him get crazy like that again. That lunatic is going to kill someone," I said.

Then a disturbing sound rumbled from the back of the wagon. "Braaaaaaaappp." That was Wally farting in his sleep. This continued like clockwork every fifteen minutes for the next three hours. We were both disgusted by the volume and length of Wally's foul extrusions. It was like a fireworks display in sound and odor. Kenny and I came up with a nickname for Wally: *"Farticus Maximus."*

Wally woke up and we commended him for the unforgettable colonic display. Wally apologized. "Sorry about all the gas. Whenever I eat Frijoles Y Arroz burritos, I'm not right for a week," he said.

We reached Phoenix. We agreed that driving would be shared amongst the three of us from this point forward. We had only 400 miles to Los Angeles. Wally suggested that he could drop us off in Santa Monica, because Santa Monica had better beaches than L.A. This was the first considerate remark Wally had made on the trip. For a moment, I thought the winds of change might be upon us.

We found our way to Santa Monica. We spotted a cheap motel—*The Tumble Inn*. This was a super low rent motel—$8 per night. It was located right across from the beach on Ocean Avenue. We got our stuff out of the Country Squire. As he was leaving, Wally stopped the Country Squire and leaned out from the driver's window. He firmly said:

"Be at this spot on Sunday at noon to get picked up. I'll wait five minutes. If you're not here, you have to find another way home. Understood?"

"Yes sir, we understand," Kenny said. "Have a great wedding Farticus." Wally's face grimaced as he gunned his Country Squire and peeled out onto Ocean Avenue.

"Wow, that guy can sure be an asshole,"I said.

"Kind of like most people," Kenny said.

Kenny and I checked into our room at The Tumble Inn. We picked up the bedspread and two towels and then went over to the beach. It was a relief to get away from Wally. As we sat on the beach, we discussed the looming drive home.

"I'm dreading the trip back. Santa Monica is like heaven. In five days we will have to endure the hell of another forty hours in a car with Wally," Kenny said.

"How about we hitch-hike back?" I said.

"Too far," Kenny said.

"I'm thinking about seeing if my mother would send me a plane ticket. How would you feel about that?" I said.

"Please don't abandon me to this insanity," Kenny said.

The next day we made our way into L.A. and spent the day at MacArthur Park, the legendary hippie playground. Some guy handed us a doobie and we officially christened our arrival into hippiedom. We mentally floated around MacArthur Park for a few hours. Checking things out. Talking with people. Smelling flowers. Observing beauty.

We went to Disneyland the next day. This felt a little childish. I wouldn't recommend it to anyone over age six.

The following day, the afternoon hours were spent on the beach. In the evening we hitched to the Sunset Strip. Despite a shortage of cash, we splurged on a couple of beers. The lavish insanity of West L.A. was on full display. For six hours we basked in the glow of ubiquitous neon lights.

Our final excursion was a meandering hitchhiking trip around the L.A. area. This was purely for the sake of adventure—no destination involved. We were picked up by a van on the south side of the L.A. basin near the Santa Monica Pier and made our way north to Brentwood. We soon found ourselves on a hilltop overlooking the L.A. metropolis while sitting beneath a Catalina Cherry Tree.

Our driver's name was Alfred Brundage. "Man, I just love it up here," Alfred said. He pulled a bottle of apple wine out of his van and handed us a doobie. "This is called lambs wool. It's from Africa," he said. Kenny and I sat down and lit it up.

The lambs wool came on strong. The African weed was potentiated by the surreal nature of the scene. The panoramic view of the valley was like a psychedelic dream. Alfred pulled a guitar out of his van and sat down with us. He played a few songs. Kenny and I became engrossed by the magnificent beauty of it all.

"I come here to meditate. As you can see, this is a very powerful place. It conveys a whole different perspective of the city, and the world. If you open your mind, the city resembles a living organism," Alfred said.

Alfred closed his eyes and paused for a few moments. Then he smiled. "Ahhh yes, the mother of the Buddha leaned against a cherry tree as she gave birth to the enlightened one," Alfred said as we sat beneath the Catalina Cherry Tree. I was deeply affected. For several months, I wondered if I should become a Buddhist.

We returned to The Tumble Inn. "Today was just what we needed," I said.

"Tomorrow, for better or for worse, we will be on the road with Wally. I could use a few more days in Santa Monica instead," Kenny said.

Sunday arrived. At 11:45 a.m. we checked out of the Tumble Inn and took a seat on a park bench to wait for Wally to pick us up at noon. By 2 p.m. Wally had not shown up yet. We agreed to give it another hour. If Wally didn't show by then the thumbs come out. The Country Squire pulled around the corner at 2:30 p.m. It was followed by a police car which parked behind Wally. Wally and the policeman both got out of their cars and approached Kenny and me.

"The officer can explain why I'm so late," Wally said.

"I'm Officer Alexander Edmond Odell, with the Los Angeles police department. Mr. Kneedirt had a mishap yesterday and we became involved. He was at a wedding yesterday and disrupted the ceremony. He was then taken to a psychiatric hospital for an evaluation. He was released about an hour ago, on the condition that he follow-through with plans to return to Kentucky. Today. Can you assure me that you will supervise his exit from Los Angeles?" he said.

We promised the officer that we would make sure that Wally left the city. We threw our stuff in the Country Squire and headed east toward Kentucky.

A few miles down the road, Wally spoke. "Okay, I'll tell you what happened. The wedding was for my ex-wife, Loretta. Not for my daughter. When the preacher asked if there was anyone who had reason to object to the wedding, I stood up and said, 'I object.'" "What is your objection?" The preacher asked. "Because Loretta is my wife," I said.

"Loretta promised to be my wife until death does us part. Then she decided to leave me after three years. She said she got a divorce, but I never agreed to it. Loretta is still my wife. She is still Loretta Kneedirt. Bigamy is still a crime in America. And you, Mr. Preacher, if you complete this ceremony, you will be committing a crime. So you better think hard about what you're doing."

"The preacher asked me to come to his office and I refused. I got really pissed off and the police showed up. The police dragged me off to a stress center. They made me stay all night. I agreed to leave town to avoid going to jail for disorderly conduct. What a crock of bull. I'm an American citizen. I have a right to free speech. This isn't Russia. This is America! They should have arrested Loretta, not me. She's a filthy Sandinista bigamist."

At that moment, I realized that Wally was even more of a lunatic than I thought.

Kenny faced Wally and said, "Let's just have an easy ride back home. Steve and I will drive. Wally, you just relax. It sounds like you've been through a lot."

"I sure have," Wally said.

"You know Wally, I was taught that some things are just not meant to be. I think of that notion sometimes when I feel disappointed," Kenny said.

"Okay Mr. Rogers. I'm going to take a nappy now," Wally said.

"That's a good choice. Pleasant dreams Farticus." Kenny said.

The trip back to Louisville was very quiet indeed. Wally was sullen and withdrawn. Kenny and I were careful to avoid agitating Wally. There was no point in discussing the wedding caper. That would have been a futile exercise—more appropriate for a psychiatrist or a probation officer. We were mostly just quiet, and asleep when possible.

We made it back to Louisville. We pulled into Kenny's parents' driveway. Kenny's mother, my Aunt Elaine, was working in her garden. She approached the Country Squire as we got out of the wagon. Aunt Elaine proceeded toward us with her friendly smile. She innocently asked,

"How was the trip boys?"

The Problem with Epictetus

I have a bone to pick with Epictetus. He lived over 2,000 years ago and left a boatload of advice on how to live. One thing troubles me in particular. He suggested that old age and decline has *"its own special gifts, if one knows how to find them."* The problem is, unfortunately, Epictetus didn't bother to tell us where to look.

Wow, I'm 69 years old right now and I've experienced a noticeable decline over the past ten years and I have found no *special gifts* in my waning physical being. Don't let Epictetus fool you. Being young is far better than being old. And here's a news flash: there is a lot of stuff that the medical system cannot cure. When I was young, I believed the common fantasy about healthcare. I believed that with enough money and brainpower, the human body could be fixed, like an automobile or clothes dryer. Get used to it, we are all going downhill. And for a lot of folks, the trip simply accelerates and ends ungracefully in the ultimate slowdown.

I've noticed that my friends and family who are now in the geriatric zone have a variety of ailments. We all say that *"when we talk, let's not get into all that medical stuff."* But we do. And we do it a lot. I vaguely remember talking about fun stuff when I was younger. Not quite so much anymore.

My communications with older folks now involve hearing about their impending double knee replacements, spots on their brain scan that their doctors are *"watching,"* and comparisons of which medications we are taking for every imaginable ailment. *"You gotta be careful with Neurontin, I hear that stuff is addictive." "You ought to try Cialis, no comparison with Viagra,""Probalan is great for gout, forget the natural stuff,"* etc., etc., etc. Also, I have gotten pictures sent to my cell phone of diabetic foot sores which resist healing leaving the afflicted person suspecting the horrifying possibility that the thing will never heal.

We have become opinionated about all aspects of medical care. We talk about how cool our doctors are and the great nurses. I don't know how the medical people put up with all of the complaining. Well, I guess that isn't true. When I was a practicing social worker I experienced a ton of emotional regurgitation from clients. The way I put up with it was by wine interventions on weekends. I can't do that anymore because alcohol doesn't go well with my medications. And reefer is out the question because it raises blood pressure.

My first serious incursion into the ravages of aging occurred at age 58. One morning I woke up with my left ear buzzing and a sense that there was a laser beam emanating from the center of my brain to the inner wall of my skull. Within a month this turned into sounds of fireworks and grinding metal in my head. I described this to my doctor and he said he had never heard of anything like that. He gave me a look that suggested he thought I was hallucinating. To move things along, I told him, *"I'm not hallucinating."* He responded, *"It sounds like Tinnitus. Usually, people hear a tiny little bell in one or both ears. Most people just get used to it. Some people say it sounds kind of like Christmas."* To me, it sounded like Christmas in hell maybe.

For me, just about everything changed. I retired early because Tinnitus interfered with my concentration and made me more irritable than normal, which was hard for some people to believe was possible.

I started on a journey through the medical system to try to cure the Tinnitus. I saw an Ear Nose and Throat specialist. He was memorable because he made no secret of his distaste for my complaining and whining. He grinned as he told me that *"there is nothing you can do about it."* I still remember his ghoulish smile.

I saw a neurologist. He told me there might be one possibility for treatment. If I had an exposed nerve near my left ear due to a damaged myelin sheath, I would need brain surgery to repair it and thus cure the Tinnitus. I felt something I never expected to feel: *excitement over the possibility of having brain surgery.* But no such luck. Surgery was not necessary. After ten years of Tinnitus, I can say that it doesn't bother me like it used to. I think of it now as *"my noisy neighbor."*

I have neuropathy which causes my legs to feel like they are in ice cold water halfway up my calves when I lay down, especially in the winter. My son Jack cuts our grass because it hurts my feet to do it myself. My prostate has gone a little crazy leaving me with intermittent pains in my *"undercarriage."* I also pee a lot. Sleep time is a peeing party. My personal record for trips to the john is seven in one night. I've become the Ted Williams of peepee.

My past injuries include, but are not limited to: falling from our attic through our family room ceiling, hitting a parked car with a motorcycle, and slipping and falling on the marble foundation of The Parthenon. These injuries have come home to roost—in the form of arthritis and generalized aches and pains.

That's just the medical part of things. Social life now is very different as well. Being old makes you feel a little invisible. When I went to the gym when I was younger, occasionally an attractive looking female would smile at me, or otherwise acknowledge my existence. In my present phase of life, that just doesn't happen. But the 75 year old ladies are cheerful and friendly. Going to the gym, or anywhere for that matter, just isn't the same.

I observe myself cheering for Joe Biden. And that is not just because he is a democrat. He is only 12 years older than me. I'm part of his club now, albeit a junior member. That guy has to feel like crap most of the time, but there he is saving the country anyway. Instead of suggesting he has dementia, people should be in awe of what he is doing, despite his age.

And of course, there is the cognition issue. I am like most people my age. We can easily remember microscopic details from events sixty years ago. But now, it is a struggle to take medication on time, remember names, and organize thinking. Conversations sometimes go like this: *"What was I saying?"* Response: *"I don't know."* I read my old bluebooks from college and I cannot believe their lucidity and creativity—weaving different subject matter together seamlessly, and sometimes with humor—and wowing my professors. I am astonished by what I used to be able to do. It is a challenge now to write even something like this little ditty. My, how things change.

But there is another type of memory problem, i.e., historical memory. Younger people do not have the same memory as older people do, simply because they weren't alive when certain things occurred. As a consequence, for example, I have stopped making references to David Niven as an exemplar of wit and charm, because about 90 percent of the time nobody knows what I'm talking about when I mention his name. Then I have to explain myself, which spoils the fun. If you don't know who David Niven was, you know what I mean.

So, young ones, my advice to you is to bask in your youth. Have awareness and gratitude for what you have. Then, when you get old you can live without regret as you search for the special gifts that Epictetus talked about. To make the search easier for you, I'll give you some ideas on where you should look for those special gifts.

The special gifts can be found in the young ones who demonstrate their naïve yet delightful wisdom by spontaneously and frequently experiencing wonder. I see my grandson, Michael, involuntarily exploding with joy and energy. I see his sister, Edith, now one month old, who magically came into this world ten months ago following a twinkle in her mommy and daddy's eyes.

I see my sons now as young men, adroitly managing their lives with grace and humor.

I see my wife and the continued love, kindness, and care she provides me after almost four decades together.

Extended family and friends provide us great happiness and the sense of a universal connection to all of humanity.

Our dogs are part of our family. They provide us a level of unconditional love, loyalty, and affection beyond explanation.

Another source of happiness is the simple truth that people are generally a lot smarter and wiser as they age. This aspect of maturity is wonderful to experience in others as well as oneself.

And finally, old age can provide the greatest gift of all: a greater appreciation of the mysterious and magical nature of the universe. This includes the awareness that each of us is a further manifestation of the design of the universe—just the same as a flower, or a tree, or a galaxy. In other words, everything is, and will be, as it was meant to be. This awareness frequently emerges as one ages and is capable of providing solace as our lives wind down.

The special gifts can certainly diminish the feeling of despair associated with aging. Thank you Epictetus, you were right about those special gifts in old age and decline —if one knows where to find them.

Grandma Hass

Lilac Road will always have a special place in my heart. My grandparents lived on that road for decades, in a small house with only two bedrooms and a couple of beautifully landscaped acres of land. This was the place my mother and her two sisters were brought up. The sisters advanced in life and established their own families, but still remained solidly in the orbit of Grandma. Throughout her life, Grandma Hass was the heart of the family. It was impossible not to love her.

Grandma Hass was the archetypal grandmother—smiling, habitually helpful, plump, wise, and a great cook. I never heard a harsh word from her. When I was a little kid my cousin Kenny caught me peeing in the back yard. Kenny quickly ran for Grandma Hass then brought her to the scene of the crime where Grandma witnessed me *"watering the grass."* She corrected me gently, *"Steven, you know that you're supposed to do that in the bathroom."* That was it. No punishment, no lecture, not even a scowl. The only evidence of displeasure was her use of my formal name, *"Steven,"* which was exclusively reserved for when I was in trouble.

Around age seven, cousin Kenny, brother Jeff, and I were given permission to *"run through the sprinkler."* I was told to put my bathing suit on in the dining room at the back of the house. Grandma walked in while I was changing. When I spotted her, I headed behind the table. *"What's wrong?"* Grandma asked. *"I don't want you to see me naked!"* I responded. *"I've seen you naked many times,"* she said. *"Oh no you haven't!"* I said. I had already forgotten that I had ever been a baby. Grandma respectfully left the room and let me finish.

Throughout the years, Grandma Hass handled communications for the family. If you wanted to know what cousin Penny had for lunch, three-hundred miles away, you could find out by calling Grandma. If Kenny had fallen out of a tree, she knew it within two hours. She routinely made calls to her adult grandchildren to stay in touch. She sent lovely little notes in the mail to cheer us up. The notes always ended in *"xoxoxo, Grandma Hass."*

Grandma was a frequent visitor to our house. She would sometimes be over the entire day to help my mother with chores. She and my mother would walk to *Russell's* market for groceries. Grandma had a little pull cart to help with transporting stuff back home. As Mom and Grandma headed out to the store, I could see Grandma limping. She fell off a ladder once when painting the chicken coop out back and broke an ankle. This resulted in permanent impairment. I always felt a little concerned seeing her walk distances. It looked painful, or at least uncomfortable. No complaining though, ever.

July 4th was celebrated at my Grandparents house. When we were younger, sparklers provided the excitement for the kids. As we got older, the older kids were allowed firecrackers. It was a miracle that none of us ever lost a finger. Besides the fireworks, Grandpa grilled out. I can still remember the thick smoke of the grill filling the back yard and mingling with the magnificent smell of burned gunpowder. Despite ambivalence about explosives, Grandma embraced the spirit of the day.

Christmas, was the big kahuna. The big family would get together about one o'clock and the festivity ended about ten o'clock. There were many rituals including a wonderful feast. Ham was the main dish along with German potatoes, dressing, and a few other side dishes. Then, wonderful homemade pies, from scratch, would appear. This was all prepared by Grandma, my mother, and two aunts. They were like a finely oiled scrumptious generating machine.

In addition to the dinner, there was a large bucket of Fannie May candy (both vanilla and chocolate buttercreams). Coca-Cola was flowing—there was no limit on Christmas. We kids were probably near pancreatic failure by the end of the celebration.

Non-food attractions included the *"fish pond."* The kids took turns sticking a fishing pole into one of the bedrooms. The older grandkids helped Grandma attach a gift to the line for the younger ones. Grandma knew how to delight us.

The toilet paper routine was a crowd pleaser. This involved unraveling a roll of toilet paper which contained dollar bills taped to the paper. A variation of this was small fake trees with money attached to the limbs. These two activities were my grandparent's method of giving their daughters and their husbands a monetary gift. It felt more meaningful than just writing a check.

My favorite was an exercise wherein Grandpa would call out: *"Everyone who kisses Grandma gets a dollar!"* The grandkids would immediately crowd around Grandma and smother her with kisses. For me, seeing Grandma in a state of rapture was the highlight of the day.

My grandparents became attached to each other starting at age fourteen. They were married in their late teens. The marriage lasted for about seventy years, until death did them part. As long as I knew them, they referred to each other as *"Mother"* and *"Daddy."* Grandma described Grandpa as *"the most wonderful man in the world."*

When I was in my mid-twenties I asked Grandma what her secret was for such a long and happy marriage. She quickly responded: *"I just learned how to keep my mouth shut sometimes."* I later became a psychotherapist and quickly realized how right Grandma was. I understood this even more after I got married.

Grandma Hass grew older and she unfortunately had a debilitating stroke. She was in a nursing home for two years. During that time, Grandpa was by her side in the nursing home for most of the day, every day. Unlike most people who are in nursing homes for two years under these circumstances, Grandma recovered enough to go home. Grandpa continued to care for her at home, which was tremendously difficult. We all got to witness true love in action.

During the last year of her life, Grandma was hospitalized three times, near death. The call went out to the family who would arrive from places near and far to see her before the end. This outpouring of love had a magical effect on Grandma. Twice she rallied and came home.

The third hospitalization was the final trip to the hospital. Family rallied, but Grandma had reached the end. In my visit with her the night before she passed away, she told me two things. The first reflected her legendary optimism: *"I'm going to get some new linoleum in the kitchen when I get home."* The other remark was stated earnestly: *"We have no control in our lives."* The second statement was more poignant and thought provoking than any guidance I received in my years studying Philosophy in college.

Grandpa passed away a few months after Grandma. My mother asked me to come over to my grandparent's house to see if I wanted any of their stuff as an inheritance. Not much was left, but two things I really cared about were still there. The first was a picture of baby Jesus. When I was a young child I would nap in my grandparent's bedroom. The picture below hung on the wall. I recall waking up from naps in a darkened room and seeing this image. Even as a child I was struck by its mystical beauty.

The other object I inherited was a *"paint by numbers"* depiction of the Last Supper which Grandma Hass had done. It hung in my grandparent's living room for many years, next to a cuckoo clock. It is a treasure to me now. I hope that one day my children will inherit these things and carry the memory of Grandma Hass forward.

What a gift for all of us to have Grandma Hass.

Eulogy for My Mother, Ardell Tyler

First of all, I would like to call to order this meeting of the Ardell Tyler Fan Club.

Otherwise, we all want to thank you all for coming today. Your support means a great deal to all of us.

The earliest memory of my mother is from around age 3. I was sick in bed and had a little cow bell that I could ring to summon her. She would quickly come up the stairs and check on me when she heard the bell. I remember that she made me French toast for lunch that day. I also remember that it was delicious.

When I was little I had a stuffed bear which I called "Kitty." Around age 4, my father decided that I was too old to have that thing, so he decided to throw poor Kitty in the trash. Of course, this was a tough moment for me, and I cried and cried. But my Mom defied her husband and pulled poor Kitty out of the trash. Kitty smelled like coffee grounds after that, but Mom still let me keep it. At that moment as a little boy, I learned that I could really count on my Mom.

During the elementary school years, I remember my mother coming home at 4 o'clock from work at the Osteopathic Hospital where she was as a nurse. She could be seen walking up 26th street to our home on Tamarac Place in Walnut Grove. She was dressed in her white uniform and starched nurses cap. She looked like an angel. I wondered how it was possible that I was related to someone so beautiful.

In regard to my mother's work as a nurse, my sister Marcia told me that she asked Mom once what Mom learned in nursing school. Mom told her simply that she *"learned to be nice."*

For example, as a nurse my mother would sometimes take a special interest in patients while they were in the hospital. After they were discharged, she would sometimes bake a pie for them and deliver it to their home as a gift. This was done quietly, without any fanfare.

One of the most wonderful qualities that Mom had was that she was an expert on everybody. She knew what people liked and she tried to get those things for them. Mom would sometimes return from shopping downtown, bringing home a dozen of my favorite Kresge's donuts and a submarine sandwich. She did the same sorts of special things for all of us.

Her thoughtfulness extended as well to evenings where Mom and my father would go out for dinner together. (By the way, dinners out away from us kids occurred certainly no more than once per year.) When it did happen, Mom would return with a portion of the dinner to share with us. We had the feeling that Mom was always thinking about us.

Sometimes in the evening Mom would sit at the dining room table by herself. She had a pad of paper and would write out the full names of her children, over and over, in cursive writing.

When we were little, every night my mother would kiss us goodnight. The kiss on the cheek was punctuated by a tremendous smacking sound right near the ear. I never really understood how she could make a sound like that. One night she told me: "I love you so much I could squeeze you to death!" This scared me a little bit but I got the message. My mother was an expert at showing people how much she loved them.

My mother was a wonderful homemaker. She kept the house spotless. Spring cleaning was celebrated annually and was a trial for young boys. There was no escape. The smell of ammonia and Windex permeated the house. I was thankful that we lived in a 900 square foot unit. A big house would have taken days to clean. We were not finished until Mom indicated that the house was sufficiently disinfected to her quality standards.

My mother was famous for her cooking and baking. Her legendary sugar cookies appeared on holidays or other special occasions. When we came home from school on Valentine's day we would find a plateful of heart shaped sugar cookies with pink frosting. They not only tasted great but they were actually just plain beautiful to look at. Christmas was of course an occasion for a cornucopia of Christmas cookies of all shapes and sizes. But as many of you know, my mother was modest. She would always deny that the cookies were very good and told us that maybe the next batch would be better.

When I went to college Mom would mail me cookies. The cookies arrived in a canister and each was wrapped individually in wax paper. I would hide the cookies away from anyone who might have the poor judgment to think I would share them. One time Mom sent a birthday cake in the mail. It was smushed but was still delicious. But what was even more wonderful than the cake was the knowledge that there was a human being in the world who cared enough about me to make that kind of effort.

On the other hand, my Mom was tough. She kept an eye on us, especially Jeff and me. One night we were camping in a tent with a couple of other boys in the field in Walnut Grove. At around 3 a.m. we decided to venture out into the neighborhood to create some havoc. As we made our way out of the tent, we heard my mother's voice yell out from her bedroom window: "Jeff and Steve Tyler get back in that tent!" We got back into the tent. I wondered if she ever slept. For several years after that night many of us referred to my mother as "Sarge."

The soft side of my Mom was reflected in another nickname. My father called Mom "Bunny." For years my cousins referred to her as "Aunt Bunny." It was a perfect nickname for someone as sweet and soft as my mother.

My mother cared about us. This extended her entire life, even until shortly before she passed away. I am told that the day before she died, she woke up and looked at those surrounding her bed and said: *"Don't be sad."* Even then, she was still taking care of us.

I am in awe at the level of kindness and generosity which permeated Mom's life. These qualities have trickled down one way or another to all of us including to those lovely little great-grand-babies sitting here today with Mom's grandchildren.

In my mind I can see Mom meeting up with my father, brother Jeff, her sisters, and her parents and having a glorious reunion.

Finally, I would like to thank my sister Marcia for taking such wonderful care of my mother not just over the past years when she was ill, but during Marcia's entire lifetime. My Mom and Marcia have always had a special bond. During the last years however, it is hard to comprehend how the time and energy Marcia spent caring for my mother was humanly possible. It is for these reasons, and others, that I have often referred to Marcia as a "giant." Just like her mother. Thank you Marcia. And thanks again to all of you for being here.

Tribute to my Father

This in memory of my father, Joseph Tyler who passed away 52 years ago. This was a gigantic loss for me and my family, one which has reverberated in many ways throughout the years. I am thankful for the 18 years he was present in my life, the lessons he taught us, and for the deep happiness he provided to my family. He was dubbed "Alexander the Great" by people who worked with him, which I think was fitting. My personal nickname for him was "The Happy Warrior," which reflected his enduring optimism in dealing with life's struggles. My biggest regret is that he did not live long enough to know my wife and my sons—a fantasy dream I have lived with for 39 years. I will always feel the sadness, for the loss of the Happy Warrior.

Joe, Jimmy, and Jack Stories

On the day that Joe was born, Susan and I got up at 5:30 a.m. for the scheduled birth. Joe was induced, being two weeks late. As we walked out to the car our neighbor, Wilbur, walked over from across the street to greet us. Coincidentally, it was his birthday also. Wilbur is an old guy and he had a sense of the weightiness of the day. As we said good-bye to him, he said: "*May God be with you today*". I got into the car and began to have some big tears roll down my cheeks. The immensity of the day had hit me. I was shocked by the amount of emotion that Wilbur's remark unleashed. Susan, being Susan, asked me if I wanted her to drive. I refused the offer. I felt that the least I could do is drive her to the hospital. I regained my composure and we finally made it to the hospital.

Susan gave birth to Joe gracefully. Despite the obvious pain that she went through, she maintained her dignity throughout. She was even intermittently checking on me to see if I was okay. When Joe came out, we both simultaneously shouted: "*It's Joe*!" It was like we had known him forever. He came out screaming like a banshee. His personality was present from the first moment. Actually, we had a sense about this child before he was born. He was a real kicker, and he moved constantly. When we brought him home, he continued to assert himself, as he does today. He is a force.

When Jimmy was born, Susan repeated her performance. I was amazed at her sweetness. Jimmy was a lot quieter than Joe, before and after birth. When he appeared, he sort of purred a little, then fell back to sleep. He has been a much more reserved and calmer child than Joe, consistent with his first moments. So, look closely when your baby is born. It will be revealing itself from the start.

* * *

Here is a little story about Jimmy. A couple nights ago I was trying to brush his teeth. Jimmy just hates that. He struggles and fights. I have to put his legs in between mine and hold his arms. He squirms and turns his head back and forth. In the middle of this ordeal, he yells out: *"Joe, help!"*, summoning help from his brother. We all cracked up. He really has a lot of faith in Joe.

* * *

Joe has been doing just fine without his pacifier. I have really been proud of him. He complained only one time, for about two minutes yesterday in the morning. Otherwise, he has just been great. He and Jimmy are watching *The Lion King* right now. They are really starting to play a lot together. Jimmy doesn't take any guff from Joe. They wrestle a lot and Jimmy holds his own. I hear him growling in the other room immitating a lion.

* * *

It is Sunday night and we are winding down here. Joe is watching "Pollyanna" and Jimmy is kind of wandering around looking for something to do. I took the boys to the McDonald's today, to the one with the huge playland, which is thrilling for Joe. On the way there he asked me if my dad used to take me to McDonald's when I was little. I told him there were no McDonald's when I was his age. He asked: *"were you sad?"* It is hard for him to comprehend that McDonalds is not timeless. But we had a great time.

* * *

Another little Joe vignette: Joe asked me one day *"if police can speed"*. I explained that sometimes they do but they shouldn't. He asked me who gives them a ticket if they speed. Then he asked me: *"Does God have*

113

rules?" I deferred that one to Susan. She told him that God makes rules for himself. I didn't think to ask that question until I was about 25. Like I said, Joe is a psychedelic experience.

Jimmy is starting to chat more and more. He tells me: *"Dad, I like you a lot"*, which is a nice thing to know. He also likes to use provocative language. He calls Joe a *"penis butt head"*, etc. He even calls me the same sometimes. He is really creative. He and Joe have a great relationship. Lots of affection punctuated by moments of primal aggression.

* * *

Having kids is also a real terrifying experience at times. For example, yesterday Jimmy felt a little hot and I took his temperature. He was 104 degrees. Scared the hell out of me. Fevers can be very dangerous to kids. Susan was sleeping to recover from the previous night's work. I got her up immediately and we began to deal with the fever. Jimmy is such a little trooper. He was just drained from the fever, but I managed to make him laugh a little. We finally got it down, and we both felt a lot better. These little guys are so innocent, it is hard to see them in pain.

* * *

Joe is becoming a man of the world. He is frighteningly charming at times. He is very outgoing, fearless, but restrained. Now Jimmy is a little more reserved, but a force unto himself. He amuses himself easily, unlike Joe who wants to play with others constantly. Jimmy also exhibits no fear of his older brother, and frequently demonstrates this.

Well, I just got the kids started in the bath. Susan is in there now because Joe refused to let me wash his little tush. He demanded that his mother do it. I didn't argue with him about it, so Susan is in there gleefully doing her duty.

114

* * *

Joe is becoming politically more astute. A couple of days ago we were seeing shots of the White House on TV. I asked Joe if he knew he lived there. Of course, he said: *"Bill"*. Then he asked me if Bill actually slept in that big house. I told him yes, and pointed out that we have had many presidents who have lived in that house. Joe then told me that he knew the name of the next president. *"Who is that?"*, I asked. *"Bill Buttmonster"*, he replied. Now this caught me a little off guard, but after a moment of thought, I figured that this description was a pretty apt nickname for our current president. Joe must know that re-election will occur. Bill Buttmonster.

* * *

Joe recently asked me why the Earth had air and why there was no air in outer space. There was also a moment where I explained to him that some people pray and they think that God can hear them. He paused for a moment and said: *"I don't think God can hear people, Dad. Do they really believe that?"* I felt a little guilty, but also a little proud at my free thinker. When Bill Clinton was on TV explaining how he got all of that soft money, Joe said: *"I think he is lying, Dad."* I asked him how he could tell. *"Because he has that funny little smile when he talks. He's lying just so he won't get into trouble."* Hmmmm.

* * *

Jimmy and I are getting closer. I am beginning to penetrate that mystical yolk between mother and son. He seems to come to me a lot now when he needs things. He is also cultivating his sense of humor. In a recent trip to South Bend, he had the family howling for about a half hour continuously. I was amazed at his capacity to entertain us. He has an instinct for the comical. We are now working on potty training. Jimmy is really not inspired yet. He has always taken his own sweet time, at about everything he does. When Jimmy eats, he eats *slowly*. Susan says, *"Jimmy doesn't eat, he dines"*.

* * *

This week Joe told me that when he grows up, he wants to live down the street, be a social worker like me, and drive to work with me in morning. We'll have lunch together, and then in the evening, he'll stop by with his kids and let Susan and me baby-sit. I asked him what he thinks his wife will be like. He said: *"She'll be nice. She'll have gray or white, or black hair"*. I then asked if there was anything else he would like her to be and he said: *"I hope she has big boobies"*. I'm beginning to think he has put a little thought into the subject.

* * *

I just said to Jimmy: *"You are so cute"*. He responded with: *"I am"*. I love that kid.

* * *

Yesterday, we got some doggie chewsticks for Sugar. Joe asked what they were made of. I told him they were made of animal skin of some sort. *"What kind of animal skin"*, he asked. I told him it was probably made from horses. He said: *"But Dad, how do you think the horses feel about being eaten?"* I am observing him becoming more aware of the feelings of others. He amazes me most of the time.

Jimmy is working on potty training. He really doesn't seem highly motivated yet. We have even gotten him a couple of great videos about using the potty and the other accompanying behaviors including washing hands. After watching one, he ran to the bathroom and wanted to wash his hands. At least he got part of it. Actually, Joe was enthralled watching the

116

videos. He thought they were great and wanted to watch them again and again. I wonder about that kid sometimes.

* * *

We will have a new baby in mid-August. Joe is very excited. This week he was asking me if girls that just became grown-ups could have babies. I told him even girls who weren't grown-ups could have babies, and he was a little surprised at this news. You can just see those wheels turning in his head. The world is a very mysterious place when you are five. Joe is also now a bit of a philosopher / sociologist. This morning we were sitting on the front lawn waiting for his Aunt Sarah to pick him up to go fishing, and he told me: *"Dad, I think the most favoritest thing people like to do is watch other people. That's what I like to do."* Joe is a psychedelic experience.

* * *

Life is going well here. Susan is expanding by the minute. The baby is a strong kicker. A Rockette with a charlie horse never kicked so much. My little guy Jimmy has been voicing some reluctance to lose his spot as baby of the family. I recently said to him: *"Do you know you are going to be a big brother soon?"* He very clearly responded with: *"I like being a baby"*. I think he knows the winds of change are blowing.

As for Joseph, he is anxiously awaiting the change. Being the oldest child, he is anxious to have another child around to play with him. He wants a boy. He is growing up. Here is a recent conversation:

Joe: *Dad, I wish you and I were brothers.*

Me: *Why do you say that?*

Joe: *So we can be together for a long time.*

117

Me: *But we will be together for a long time.*

Joe: *But you are going to die before me.*

Me: *Well, I hope so. But even if I die, we will always be together.*

Joe: *We will?*

Me: *I will always be in your heart. And besides that, did you know that half of you is made from me and half is made from mommy. So I will always be with you in that way too.*

Joe: *You mean like those little worms that try to get into that big peach?*

Me: *Yes Joe.*

* * *

I had a conversation with Joseph after his first fishing expedition. He went fishing with his Grandfather Gallagher recently.   When he returned, we had this conversation:

"Dad, you wanna hear about the fish I caught?"

"Sure." I said.

"I caught huge, tons of fish. I caught a monster fish. It weighed as much as a car. Did you ever think a fish could weigh so much?"

"That's amazing, Joe". I said. *"Do you think you want to go fishing again?"*

"Yeah, Dad. I'll teach you."

This is not a fictional conversation. Joe is a miracle. He does teach me things, all the time.

* * *

Jimmy is coming into his own. He still speaks his own language. For example, his pronunciation of *horsie* is *hor-tee*. He still jibbers sometimes, but he does it *in earnest*. He also claims that his name is *Joe*. He is a scrapper. He sort of manhandles Joe sometimes. He is getting big too. He is sweet.

* * *

A couple of weeks ago, my mom, Marcia, and the girls were down. We went down to the canal downtown and rented a paddle boat for the kids. I watched them as they paddled. At one point I looked back and Joe had fallen into the water. My niece, Megan, pulled him out. Joe has a way of making things like that happen. A couple of months ago he jumped off the couch and a rod from a tripod jammed into his nose, where the nose meets the eye, requiring 13 stitches. We are very lucky it didn't hit the eye. A plastic surgeon had to be called in. By the end of his fifth year, Joe has had 18 stitches, and one concussion. This summer, he also had a bike wreck which resulted in multiple contusions, bruises, and a goose-egg on his forehead the size of half a baseball. We didn't even bother to take him to the hospital for that one, even though I think we probably had good reason to. I think we were just getting tired of going to the hospital.

* * *

Jimmy on the other hand has never had an injury. He is careful. I think he gets caught up in watching Joe too, which may keep him out of trouble. Otherwise, Jimmy is a comedian. He is a mime. He entertains us by running around making faces and speaking imaginary, nonsensical words. He is unique.

* * *

Joe: "*Dad, remember that night you threw the beanie baby against the wall cause you were mad?*"

Dad: "*Yes.*"

Joe: "*Remember I cried real hard?*"

Dad: "*Yes.*"

Joe: "*That was when I loved toys.*"

Dad: "*You don't love toys anymore?*"

Joe: "*No. That was before I learned my lesson that toys aren't alive.*"

* * *

One evening Joe had been misbehaving quite a bit. He had a total of five time outs from the dinner table alone. All evening we all had been on Joe quite a bit for bugging us and otherwise misbehaving. So by snuggle time (right before bedtime when we all get into bed together) Joe was pretty upset. He said we were all acting like we didn't like him. I pointed out that he had been pretty bothersome all evening and maybe that was the reason we were on his case. At that point, Jimmy said to Susan: "*Mom, you my treasure.*" Susan was very touched by this display of affection. Jimmy turned to me and said: "*Dad, you my treasure too.*" I was similarly touched. Then Jimmy slowly turned to Joe and said: "*Joe, you **not** my treasure*". At which, Joe turned away, sobbing wildly. Jimmy smiled as big as day.

* * *

I was out in the garage, briefly, when I heard Joe say to Jimmy: "*Don't tell Dad*". I came in the kitchen and asked Joe, "Don't tell Dad *what?* At which, Joe said, "*Nothing*". Upon further questioning, Jimmy eagerly pointed out that Joe had marked on the wall paper with a pencil. Well, this was Joe's third offense for marking on the walls, so he was placed in one hour time out. After about one half hour, Joe stopped me in the hallway, and requested a reduction in sentence. I adamantly refused and said: *"You're in time-out, don't even talk to me right now."* Jimmy was standing nearby and said: *"You the best dad in the whole world!"*

* * *

Joe is now seven. He is doing great in school. We have tremendous conversations. Here is one we had about President Clinton recently:

Joe: *"What did the president lie about, Dad?"*

Me: *"Well, it's kind of grown up stuff, you know? Besides that, it is kind of hard to explain."*

Joe: *"Well, I have plenty of time, and if I don't understand something, I will tell you and you can just explain it a little better for me."*

Me: *"Well, I don't think so."*

Joe: *"Come on, Dad."*

Me: *"Well, the president lied about having a girlfriend, besides his wife."*

Joe: *"What! He had a girlfriend?" You mean like the kind you kiss and stuff?"*

Me: *"Yeah."*

Joe: *"That must have made his wife feel bad."*

Me: *"I guess so."*

Joe: *"And that's why they want to kick him out?"*

Me: *"Yup."*

121

Joe: *"I don't think that's fair."*

Me: *"Why?"*

Joe: *"That would be like if I did something wrong and you gave me a time out and made me stay in my room forever."*

My little democrat.

* * *

Jack is expanding by the minute. He is the cutest baby, and sweet too. We are having so much fun with him. The boys are crazy about him too. Joe says he "can't wait until we find out what Jack is really going to look like" (when he gets older). Jimmy calls him "my Jack." They have a little love affair going, as we all do.

* * *

Susan is snoozing, since she worked last night. The boys are watching *The Three Stooges*, which they love. By the way, I taught Joe the rules for Chess yesterday, and today he actually beat the computer one game. He held me off in a match for about 15 minutes. He is definitely a *pentium*. As for Jimmy, I am enclosing his latest art work, which I think is definitely *avant garde*! Take a look:

Note the effective use of belly buttons on each person. Jimmy has a unique way of doing about everything.

* * *

Here is a conversation with Jimmy, age 5:

Jimmy: *"Dad, I like to cuss."*

Me: *"You do?"*

Jimmy: *"Yeah."*

Me: *"What do you like about cussing?"*

Jimmy: *"Oh, cussing at people."*

Me: *"You know you can get in trouble for cussing?"*

Jimmy: *"I know."*

* * *

Well, to the boys. Joe, at age seven, says to me: *"Have you ever thought that the world might be just a little ball on the finger of a big giant, and that we don't know it because we are so little?"* I was twenty-two before that crossed my mind. Later he said: *"Was there ever a time when there was nothing, not even space?"* Of course, I had not had that thought until my mid-twenties either. I wonder what *he* will think about when he is in his mid-twenties. I am afraid to consider it.

Jimmy is my happy go lucky little guy. He is enjoying piano training and doing quite well. When we were at Uncle Kenny's funeral, he saw me have a tear and he quietly came over and hugged me. He didn't say a word. It was just what I needed. I love him dearly.

Jackie boy is under the weather right now with a cold. He actually snuggled me for about twenty minutes the other night. Usually, he lasts about eight seconds on your lap, before he is off to investigate something or other. He is *driven!* He is going to be something to watch. He is already.

* * *

One day in the car we had this conversation, Joe age 7, Jimmy age 5:

Jimmy: *Dad, do things change?*

Dad: *Sure, everything changes.*

Joe: *You mean everything changes?*

Dad: *Sure. It may not seem like it, but if you waited long enough, everything would change.*

Joe: *I can think of something that does not change.*

Dad: *You can. Okay, what never changes?*

Joe: *(Pauses) Well, the right way to spell a word never changes.*

Dad: *I guess you're right.*

* * *

At bedtime one night, Joe was looking at a pillow made by Grandma Tyler, a Christmas present:

Joe: *Did Grandma really make this?*

Dad: *Sure.*

Joe: *Gee, she can do so many things.*

Dad: *She sure can.*

Joe: *But the best thing she knows how to do is **love**.*

* * *

Joe at bedtime, almost 8 years old:

Joe: *Dad, I'm just so happy to be alive!*

Dad: *What do you mean?*

Joe: *It's all so wonderful!*

* * *

Joe, almost 8 now:

Joe: *I know what sex is mom.*

Mom: *Oh, you do. What is it?*

Joe: *It is when you take all your clothes off, and kiss somebody.*

Mom: *Well, I think you are just about right.*

Joe: *Have you ever had sex?*

Mom: *Well...yes, I guess I have.*

Joe: *With who?*

Mom: *With your father!!!*

Joe: *Oh.*

* * *

Jimmy won a goldfish at the state fair this week. Of course, it died in about four days. It died yesterday, and it was still in the tank this morning. Jimmy told me this morning: *"I think I'll go check and see if my goldfish is still dead."* Ah, to be five years old again!

* * *

Recently at bedtime:

Jimmy: *Dad, I never want you to die.*

Dad: *Oh, I have a long way to go. By the time I leave, you guys will be so sick of me that you'll be happy to see me go.*

Joe: *Dad, we could never feel that way.*

What a joy it is to be loved by these boys. Here is the truth: *it is the kids who have the unconditional love, not the other way around.*

* * *

One morning, I was summoned to get a tiny spider off the ceiling. Jimmy enthusiastically said: *"Dad's not afraid of anything!"* What an honor to be the father of these boys!

Joe had another basketball game today. He scored his first point of the season. He smiled as big as the solar system when it happened. I was nearly ecstatic myself. He also got into a jump-ball situation, resulting in our team getting possession of the ball. I was proud of him for that too. In general, our team is a little too polite. They are all good boys who have been taught

126

not to grab things from people. This is especially true for Joe. So, on the court, they politely let the ball go to the other team. Joe even called the other team *"ball hogs"* because they kept dominating things. So we are trying to give them permission to be more grabby on the court, contrary to their training at home. In the end today, we lost the game. The loss was incidental in light the glory of Joe's first basket.

* * *

I took the boys to Kittles furniture store the other night. The salesman asked Jimmy if he ever hits his little brother. Jimmy replied: *"I kick him in the nuts."* So afterward, we went to a McDonald's with a playland. Jimmy spontaneously stands up in the middle of the play area, faces all the adults, extends his private area--pointing to it with both hands and bouncing on his tippy-toes--and says: *"My pee-pee, my pee-pee. My pee-pee, my pee-pee. My pee-pee, my pee-pee. My pee-pee, my pee-pee."* At first the adults all looked very concerned, then they cracked up. I stated to the audience: *"The civilizing process takes a very long time, as you can tell."* Jimmy was unphased. In a strange way, I felt very proud of Jimmy at that moment.

* * *

In light of the death of Susan's grandmother, I was reminded how tenuous and short life is. Grandma Jedinak had a long life, but somehow it just doesn't ever seem *long enough*. At the funeral, Joe cried as the family gathered around the casket for a final viewing. He is so sweet. I gave him some kleenex, and he said: *"Thanks, Dad."* So grown up at eight years old. This was a poignant moment. At times like that I realize how connected we are. Jimmy chose not to witness the funeral scene. I respect and admire him for his judgment. Some things we just don't need to think about, especially at age 6.

127

* * *

Passing by the living room one day, I hear Jimmy and Jack. Jimmy says to Jack: *"You got the cutest face I ever seen."* *(Jimmy age 6, Jack 2)*

* * *

When I heard a disturbance in the back yard, I thought Sugar might have cornered the raccoon. I grabbed Joe's baseball bat, just in case. Joe, my young humanitarian, says: *"Dad, if you get blood on that bat, you have to buy me a new one."*

* * *

Jimmy, age 6: Dad, do you still feel sad 'cause your dad died?

Me: Yeah, I do.

Jimmy: You still miss him?

Me: Yep. I do.

Jimmy: I miss him too. Well, you still got your mom.

Me: Yes I do, don't I.

* * *

I want to let you know that Joe uttered the following words to me the other night, after the American League playoff game. These words have been spoken by countless other boys to their dads. He said: *"Dad, someday when I grow up I want to play for the Yankees."* This was a sweet moment for a baseball-loving daddy.

* * *

No progress on the potty-training front. Jack refused to wear underwear this morning. Why?—you might ask. He says that underwear is now "too dangerous." After he said this, he laughed, so he knows he isn't putting anything over on me.

* * *

Grandma Greiner and the grandkids were considering where to go on their next Ambassadair trip. One option was New York City. Shopping for four hours was the primary activity of the trip, to which Joe objected. *"Shopping is a weakness,"* he said. I am proud of him.

* * *

The boys and I have been on a James Bond 007 film fest for the past two weeks. I had forgotten how great those flicks are. We are watching the Sean Connery titles only. I am amazed at how tame they are, despite the impression in the 60's that they were so racy. I am quite comfortable letting my little guys watch. Last night in one scene, Jill St. John appeared in bra and panties. Jack says: *"I like that lady. Let's go to she's house."* I said, *"Sounds good to me."*

* * *

Jack (age 4) recently announced that he has decided he is going to start being a "good boy." I think he is figuring out the good boy approach seems to work better for him. I see him growing up a little too fast. In fact the other night, we watched a show about a mother giving birth to a new little baby, and I felt kind of sad. I realized that those days are gone for me. Jack is getting to a point where he doesn't quite seem little anymore.

* * *

One little story about Jack. Recently, I was trying to get him moving to get dressed and out of the house. I was playing with words a bit, trying to sound like an Old English speaker, and said: "Let's goeth, Jacketh." Jack responded: *You jackass.* I think he thought I said jackass when I said "Jacketh." He cracks me up, a lot. Now, if *I* would have said "jackass" at age four, there would have been an inquisition, followed by burning at the stake. Things change.

* * *

It is Saturday morning, and I just got back from the coaches meeting at First Baptist to begin the new baseball season. I will be Jimmy's coach, our team is the Red Sox. I am looking forward to an exciting season, as usual. The First Baptist League is renowned for encouraging sportsmanship over competition which I support strongly, especially at this tender age. Jimmy spontaneously came up to me this morning and gave me a hug as a thank-you for being his coach. He's my sweetheart.

* * *

We took the kids to the circus last week, which turned out to be a fiasco. We got there late, ended up sitting in the last row at Conseco Field House, which was a particular problem for me because I can't see long distances very well anymore (or short ones for that matter). The performers looked like ants. Jack actually fell out of our aisle into the seats below and landed on a little girl, upsetting her mother. The performance itself was weak, compared to the mesmerizing Barnum and Baily Circus we saw two years ago. (This was the Sheffield Brother's Circus.)

The highlight of the circus was when the three elephants in the middle ring pooped simultaneously, resulting in an eruption of laughter and cheers from the crowd. The elephants must have sensed their triumph, because they immediately began to pee all over the middle ring. The crowd cheered

130

wildly again! At the end of the show, the human cannonball was fired. Afterwards, Jack looked at me and said: *"Why did they do that?"* I had no answer for him. The circus wasn't quite what we had hoped for. In fact, Jimmy calmly stated: *"I will never go to a circus again."*

* * *

Jimmy at age 12 now has a girlfriend, Lexi.

Dad: *What do you like about Lexi?*

Jimmy: She's *funny, and she's nice to me, and she's smart, and she doesn't get into trouble.*

I was 31 years old before I took on that sort of attitude.

* * *

Joe, age 14:

Joe: *"Music is a big part of my life."*

Dad: *As well it should be.*

* * *

Jack, age 8:

"Dad, I hope we never win the lottery. I mean, if we won it we would probably stop doing a lot of things like taking walks and we would pay people to do things for us that we like to do. I like things just the way they are."

We are doing something right.

131